*For Laura*

# Daybook

*Daybook.*



First published in Great Britain in 2024 by Splice,
54 George Street, Innerleithen EH44 6LJ.



Paperback Edition: ISBN 978-1-9196398-8-8
eBook Edition: ISBN 978-1-9196398-9-5

# Daybook

Nathan Knapp

SPLICE

THE AUTHOR wishes to thank Lewis Freedman, J.C. Hallman, Dan Lane, Daniel Davis Wood, and Laura Grafham Knapp.

*A writer's "sources"? His shames*

— Emil Cioran

Earlier today, as we were driving along the spine of a ridge with a far view to the north of that steep range of low mountains I have known all my life, and which I to this day think of as my mountains, my papa said to me that his son, my uncle, had told him that he wanted his ashes scattered here on the day of the first snow of the year after his death. I asked him when his son said this. Four or five years ago, he said. Wonder how he feels about it now. A moment later he pointed his red finger at some steel beams standing upright in a level part of the pasture just below us, eight rusted poles equidistant from one another, four to a row. Those my papa said were going to be for the barn. He'd planned to build a house nearby. When I asked him why he didn't my papa said: I guess he decided he wanted to do something else. We were deer hunting from the comfort of one of his several white trucks, my first time hunting at all in close to fifteen years, the pickup crawling from pasture to pasture, rising and falling through mare's tails and tall reddish sage grass, from open hayfield to darkened thicket at the speed of three or four miles an hour, the sky above us heavy with clouds, the fading light the color of blood in a bruise. My papa's green-stocked 6.5-millimeter Creedmoor lay muzzle-down against the floorboard between us, below the barrel of which rested two cardboard cartons of different caliber cartridges, neither very heavy, each containing twenty or thirty .17 or .22-250 caliber ballistic tips, which cartridges I'd just inspected following an anecdote in which my papa related, with muted but obvious satisfaction, the brief but happy story of how he'd recently used one to blow an unsuspecting turtle completely apart. We came out of the thicket and into another pasture. My papa pointed again and told me the name of the man who owned the land beyond the fence to our left. Like the names of most of the people who make their lives in these woods where my papa was raised and where he raised his daughter and son and where his daughter raised me, the name he mentioned was familiar but brought to mind no face, and though he continued to speak about some relative of the man, who may well have been a distant relative of ours—nearly everyone from this town is related to everyone else either by blood or marriage (or both) by at least the third or fourth generation back (three of the first four crushes I had were on first, fourth, and third cousins respectively)—I no longer heard him, for I was thinking instead of a particular misty morning when as a young boy I'd watched his son shoe a horse, recalling the rough sound of file against hoof, the sharp tink of hammer on nail, the sweetish scent of horse and horse saddle and horse hay and horse shit and the cans of light beer he drank and tossed to rattle in the back of his truck: how, I wondered that morning, as I still wonder now, could a creature willingly endure having a nail driven into its body? I knew of only one other exemplar of such willing endurance. Even He, much to my bafflement, being that He was God, or so I'd been repeatedly taught and at that time thoroughly believed, that final night in Gethsemane, deserted by his lazy disciples, had not exactly welcomed the idea. Let this cup pass from me He said to God (Himself) but God (Himself) did not oblige Him—and then His friends fled before the approaching mob. So abandoned, Christ gave himself up to the trial of the Sanhedrin and the ambivalence of Pilate and then the public whipping and the nails, and it thus transpired, watching him drive nails into a horse, that I came to suspect him of something. Of precisely what I was not sure. All I knew was that he was my mother's brother, and that he was taller and he laughed, on those occasions when he laughed, louder than anyone else, and that though the perpetual cast of his face belonged to his father, it was colder, twisting into a smile that looked kind on the elder and made the younger man appear cruel. In the truck, crossing the black water of a shallow creek, my papa laughed softly to himself. He was now talking about a recently dispatched coyote—two syllables: *kai-yoat*. I punched *him*, he said. My uncle was always something other. Now, writing this, I see that what I perceived then as his otherness was that unlike the rest of us, he was *his own*. He wasn't God's, like I was and my parents were, or so I was told. He wasn't my papa's or granny's or mother's, either, though they were of course related by blood. He was his own and it was through this, through his *ownness*, or so I now think, writing the initial version of this paragraph in the house where I spent the bulk of my childhood, on the night of the twenty-second day of the eleventh month of the year after hunting this afternoon with my papa, his father—it was through this fact of being his own and no one else's that he came to emanate that immense solitude which I detected in him even then, when I was but five or six years old, watching him drive nails into a horse's hoof. Another time, one evening at dusk at the high school where my papa worked as a maintenance man, after I'd been forbidden to do so, while my papa wasn't paying attention to me, I watched him pull a sinister metal mask down over his face and take up a torch that spouted a strange blue fire and sent sparks in all directions. Seeing me look my papa said: Don't look. You'll go blind. (How I wanted to look! I wanted to look and keep looking.) My uncle welded and shoed horses and branded cows and drank beer and his wife took me riding and smoked in the pickup on the way to the rodeo arena and I never quite knew, other than her name, who she was. One night near the arena during the yearly rodeo I saw her then-husband drinking with my papa's brother and some other men I did not know, or did not really know: their laughter, in the shadows behind the bleachers where I went to sit with my papa, erupted from some deeper and darker place in the body than the laughter of any of the men in my father's family, or so I then thought. (When, I asked my papa, was the bullriding? You'll see, he said.) They separated and later divorced and afterward I saw him less and less and have not seen her since, though their names remain beside each other on a certain headstone I know, which stands over the remains of my papa's father and mother. Now, when I see him, my uncle, at ever lengthening intervals of years, even across one of the linoleum-covered tables at the café, it is as if we are looking at each other from the opposite sides of a vast pasture. He begins to speak and doesn't. I begin to speak and don't. At last he cannot put it off any more and he opens his mouth and his voice sounds as simultaneously familiar and strange to me as the shadows thrown by the lights of the rodeo arena glimpsed almost three decades ago. How've you been, he says. Though I have never once called him by his real name, he calls me by mine, which no one uses anymore. Scatter my ashes, he said, here, on the day of the first snow of the year after my death, while my papa and I drove from pasture to pasture, dense thicket to empty hayfield, and I looked up at those mountains I call my mountains, here in southeast Oklahoma—home—before I sat down to write the initial version of these words on the night of the twenty-second of November in the house where I was raised. Don't look, he said again, more emphatically this time. Don't look.

I see now that there was a question my uncle raised in me that took me a very long time to ask of myself, a question never fully expressed in words because I never doubted the answer, which was given to me over and over again throughout my childhood: to whom did *I* belong? First and foremost, or so I was told, to God. After Him, to my father and mother. What I glimpsed in my uncle was a different answer to the same question and it was precisely this that made him both who he was and thus fundamentally unknowable. That he was his own, and the immense solitude which resulted from this, though I did not have the words to express it until tonight, writing the initial version of this paragraph and the one above, the first two of this writing, was the true source of my childhood suspicion of him, or so I now think, writing this, sitting there in the barn on the short stool with the horse's hoof propped up on his knee, a fine mist falling just beyond the barn door. Don't ever stand behind a horse, he said. He's liable to kick you. Why, I said. Because he can't see you there, he said, and if he can't see you, he doesn't know what you are.

The sun is going down now over the ridge to the south, a different ridge from the one mentioned in the first paragraph of this writing, on my left, brush-covered, in more or less the same place that the moon went down last night. Through park-like woods behind me stands the house in which I grew up and in which I last night wrote the initial versions of the above paragraphs. Every now and then as I write I can hear the voices of my son and Elle in the yard, playing on the swing-set behind the house. Directly across the pond from where I sit towers a darkness of pines along a fence-line built by my father and his father more than twenty years ago, during a period of my father's father's madness. Beyond the pines flows the river, invisible from where

I sit writing these words. A timber company planted these fast-growing conifers forty-odd years ago; when my grandfather bought the land for some two hundred dollars an acre in the early 1980s they were near their prime and ready to be cut. Now they are old for their kind, thick in their planted ranks. Most of the local buzzard population roosts together every night just beyond the pine plantation, in the mixed hardwoods that resume a dozen or so yards from the riverbank, high in a pair of bone-white sycamores at the mouth of a shallow inlet about two hundred yards from where I now sit, the carrion-eaters congregating in the dusk together above the shallow water, poking out the obscenity of their naked necks from within their black feathers as men's dongs once extruded from dirty trench coats in the days of blue cinemas. In the early nineties, in the madness of his mid-sixties, my father's father briefly thought he could fix himself by becoming a cowboy, a bizarre turn of events seeing as he hated cowboys more than anything else in the world, and it was then that he and my father built the fence, in what remains a concrete expression of his personality which he seems to have passed onto me: the gift or curse of mistaking metaphorical realities for material ones and vice versa. Shortly after he and my father built the fence that phase of his madness subsided and, though still attached to a few pines here and there, the fence itself rusted and fell into disrepair, and remains a monument to the rusting and falling into disrepair of his mind. (In such places as this one, in these woods for instance and along this river, where to abandon an idea often means to leave behind physical evidence of an internal wound, there are moments when to mistake the material for the metaphorical, as it turns out, may be no mistake at all.) Instead of running cows we went crow hunting. We, meaning he and his brother and my father and I, on what few good days in those years he had. He owned a battery-powered black box with a speaker into which one could insert a tape recording of the sounds of crows speaking to one another excitedly, much in the same tone as the ones I heard just now in the pines as I was writing the initial version of the previous sentence. One could turn on this box and then, if so inclined, the crows would come and, if so inclined, one could shoot at them (they were, and did; we were, and did). Just now I heard my son through the park-like woods behind me let forth a shriek. That swing-set behind the house, where my son just shrieked, was my father's father's final project, spurred on by the urging of his last remaining friend on one of his last remaining friend's final visits. The only thing I knew about his friend was that they had known each other since they were boys together, as it seemed to me several centuries earlier, and that his friend was an oilman and, as such, quite rich. The boy isn't shrieking anymore. I think he's okay.

Once we went to stay at the oilman's magnificent house and it was there, fearfully and for the first time and well before I ever desired to do so, that I slept with a girl. The purpose of our visit, if I recall correctly, was a funeral, in that county in the central part of the state where the oilman, my grandfather, and my father were all born. The fact of their having been born amidst that landscape, so altogether different in its particularities from the one in which I myself had been born and where we lived, imparted to it a mythic quality: in the far-flung pastures, the sweeping distances between the small stands of scrubby and brush-choked blackjacks, I imagined I saw the land of my true origins—the land of my father and his father and his father's father—where there were no mountains and no cowboys that I knew of, only hills that rolled gently to the horizon as if blown there by the wind, where all my father's old people either were from or kept, held in the various old person's homes that to my mother's horror I could not help referring to as funeral homes, in that place where everyone knew my father's father and my father, and where, conversely, my mother and I had to be introduced—yes, here's my daughter-in-law, this is my grandson—in that county where I stepped into the largest house I'd ever seen, the oilman's, and was shown to a room down a long hallway on the second floor, in which above the fireplace hung something I'd never before seen: an oil painting of a girl of about my own age or perhaps a few years younger, whose eyes looked down at me and which produced a sensation I very much did not like, for I detected in her expression a certain envy, possibly because she was trapped there in the painting whereas I was not. I told myself she was not alive. She's not alive, I said to myself a second time, but there could be no debate: alive or not, while in that room, no matter where I stood or sat or lay, her eyes never left me, and I was sure that when it was time for bed and I was condemned to sleep alone in that room with her that she very well might take her revenge for her lack of freedom. Just now a silent crow passed overhead and disappeared into the pines, heading in the direction of the unseen river.

It was when I was around my son's age that I began to suspect that my whole life was being clandestinely filmed, though I did not know who they, the ones filming me, were. I did know, however, that they did not have permission to do so, and suspected, because they never showed themselves, that their motives might not be pure. One explanation for my initial suspicion is innocent enough. Even at that age I grasped, rightly I think, that there was no such thing as pure fiction, only real events caught on film or described in written words. (How could I think otherwise? We read the Bible every day and believed that in it were described real and true events.) If so, or so I logically assumed, all films must be made by hidden cameras. And yet the natural result of this thought belied a darker possibility, which caused me to worry that there might exist a fiction either beyond or in front of the real events of my life, namely that if my life were being filmed on the sly, or, even more disconcertingly, if my life was a film that had already been made, then it became possible that my father was not merely my father—if indeed he was my father—but rather a villain in disguise. (There were moments when he, like my uncle, rather than *ours*, seemed like his own.) This particular thought startled me one night when I woke in the passenger seat of his pickup truck as it rumbled along the rutted dirt road toward the cabin where we lived, which was owned by a man called Fears and as such called the Fears Cabin or Fears Place. It was so dark I could not see the man driving the truck. I assumed naturally enough that this man was my father but for one detail, which did not square with the image of the man I knew. There was something on fire in his mouth. I had seen other men with something on fire in their mouth but never my own father. And yet, waking, there he was, or rather someone was, driving the darkened truck with something on fire in his mouth. To make matters stranger still, when I recall this memory to mind, I am seated on his right and the truck is headed not toward, but away from the cabin. Gradually as I now observe the memory to its conclusion he begins to look more and more like my father and there the memory ends, for when I saw him for himself my alarm ceased. That night when the light was turned out I could not see the girl in the painting but I knew she was there. She took no revenge on me, but I remember waking the next morning with palpable relief at having made it through the night, my first with a member of the opposite sex not my mother nor sisters, and that at the breakfast table in the oilman's house I was astonished to glimpse through the windows of that room a pasture that stretched farther than any I'd ever seen, with cows upon cows grazing there beneath a yellowish sky. As we ate breakfast a heavy rain began to fall beyond the high windows of the oilman's dining room, a flash of lightning lit the pasture, and thunder boomed so loudly the panes rattled, causing my younger sister to scream, at which the oilman and my father's father laughed. Writing this, I now somewhat doubt that we were there for a funeral, but also cannot imagine out of all the memories of my childhood for what occasion we would have stayed the night in that county where my grandfather and his son my father were born, other than to see someone buried.

Now that I've finished the initial version of the above paragraph, I can see it, that trip's ultimate destination: the cemetery of a town called Holdenville. Unlike most other cemeteries I knew in those of my life's earliest days, most but not all of the headstones here were set directly in the ground, their faces to the empty sky. The funeral was that of my father's father's youngest brother, his half-sibling, whom I never knew, and the wind blew as it never blew beneath those mountains I still think of as my mountains throughout the entire graveside service without stopping even for a moment, which made it hard to hear the words of the preacher standing next to the casket. (It's possible that my recollection is incorrect, and I am conflating one funeral or even cemetery with another. I do not know.) Every day a man called Mr. Gates drove past the Fears Place and every day I ran out of the house and shot him. Some days he would raise thumb and point index finger and shoot back, or make as if I'd got him. My bed stood in a corner of the living room, in the center of which was a wooden pole, which presumably held up the roof, which leaked into two or three of my mother's cooking pots every time there came a heavy rain. Now, there are times when, in writing this, my father still sits on the sofa next to my bed cleaning his .50-caliber black powder rifle, a Hawking, while I play with his shoelaces. My mother tells me Mr. Gates is driving by and I leave off writing and quit the shoelaces and run out of the house and kill him. But I now see that Mr. Gates cannot be driving by. Not if my father is cleaning his gun, or so I now see in revising the words which have come to form the substance of this memory, for my father only cleans his guns at night before hunting the following morning—so I do not run out of the house. Instead I look up at my father. Soon he will hoist me in his arms and flash the wire stubble of his cheek against my softer face. Finished with the gun and its sharp-smelling oil, he places it back in its case and fries eggs and sausage and toast, and lets me have a few bites before bed. Something about this food is strange and wonderful to me—most likely because it, unlike all the other food I eat, is made by him. When he takes me in the dizzying heights of his arms I feel like he may as well be God: thus is one of the greatest confusions of the first two-and-a-half decades of my life inaugurated. In the morning he is already gone hunting by the time I wake and Mr. Gates drives by and I shoot him as always but the wound, as usual, is not fatal, for he laughs and crosses the cattleguard and his rickety old flatbed truck winds slowly out of the pasture to the gate at the far end, where a small figure exits the truck and opens the gate, returns to the truck, drives past the gate, then gets out again and closes the gate. (The figure is no longer Mr. Gates because Mr. Gates is dead.) One morning in the spring before Mr. Gates drives by I run down the short hallway to wake my father, and when I pull back the sheets, yelling wake up, wake up, to my horror I find attached to him, surrounded by a forest of shockingly dark hair already hosting a few silver strands, the augury of some dark knowledge belonging either to the future or past or both. Don't look, my papa said.

Earlier today I visited the cemetery where I hope one day to have a headstone with my name on it, which I have made a habit of visiting ever since I first left this place for college in the northwest. It lies near the end of a narrow old road, paved at some point in the past century, in the center of which grows a strip of emerald moss, for the road itself, bordered on either side by post oaks and gnarled cedars stitched together by barbed wire, lies almost always in shadow. A stand of dense brush crowds beyond the left-hand fence-line. On the other side a rocky pasture climbs up towards the woods at the peak of the hill. At the top of a gentle rise the road opens out to a small dirt lot with a far view of the mountains on the left and the cemetery on the right, the cemetery itself level in the near part and slowly sloping up the hill in the back, bordered on all sides by a chain-link fence. The place has the air of an extinction event prolonged, endured, and—beyond all probability—sustained. The first grave I found this afternoon was that of my great-grandfather and great-grandmother, their joint-headstone affixed with the names of their twelve children, one of which belongs to my mother's mother, who grew up in a small house about two miles as the crow flies or does not fly from where I sit writing these words by the pond. Just now I heard two gunshots from separate directions as I type this with increasingly cold hands. The sun is gone now behind the ridge.

Where, I asked myself as I walked through the cemetery, would I want to be buried, were I to be buried here? I thought about my mother's mother, in that tiny house with her twelve siblings, her name etched among all those others on the stone that stood just a few feet away. I thought about her daughter, my mother. It was when I was around the same age as that of the event mentioned at the end of the paragraph above the paragraph above this one when one morning at the Fears Place I saw her in a mysterious and terrifying state. I had just entered the house from its only doorway, letting the screen bang shut behind me. As it banged she shouted my name at the top of her lungs. Naturally I ran in her direction, through the living room, down the short hallway, and into the room she shared with my father, where I arrived just as she completed her sentence: DON'T COME IN HERE. There she was, in the closet on my right: her back turned, all of her, naked. I ran terrified from the room, the sound of her laughter chasing me to my little bed. When she emerged, clothed, she laughed at my expression and reassured me that I'd done nothing wrong. Another report came over the hill as I wrote the previous sentence. *Pohhhhh.* It would be almost twenty years before I would again flee the presence of a woman in such a way, only a few months after getting married in Seattle. The young woman in question and I met up with a group of friends at a quiet bar on top of Queen Anne Hill, but for some reason I no longer recall, our friends failed to stay long, leaving behind just the two of us, or four of us if you counted the two very prominent features of her anatomy below her clavicular area which I could not help thinking of as magnificent and which, though I certainly did not count them as persons, I could not prevent from causing my heart to pound—indeed, or so I said to myself there in the bar as the young woman and I talked, in all the days of my life up to that point I'd rarely enjoyed the opportunity to be in such close proximity to two such genuine feats of human anatomical glory, nor found such entities to belong to such a funny person, especially one who seemed to enjoy talking with me as much as I was enjoying talking with her, and so it was natural enough for me to want to buy us both another round, but I was too terrified to discover what might happen if I did, knowing that another round can lead to another round and *who knows what* after that—of course I knew what—as if by buying us both another drink (drinks) this ambiguous-specific thing which I feared would happen *would* happen, guaranteeing that my whole life would unravel there on the very spot—as if those entities of hers might somehow bop their way out of her shirt and get me in a chokehold or something, and I must now admit, even if I did not allow myself to admit it that night, writing this, that there would've been many much worse ways to die—and so instead of buying her a drink and me a drink I said I had to go and sprinted down the steep south side of the hill from the quiet bar toward the apartment I shared with the woman I'd married only a few months before, running as fast as my legs would carry me and nearly falling flat on my face several times in the dark, trying to outpace what I thought was my sin but was actually only a part of myself, the part of myself that deeply, badly wanted to know—but which also, in a crucial sense, did not allow me to admit to myself that I wanted to know—what lay on the other side of the commitment I'd made to my wife after barely two decades on earth, to find out the kinds of things that could happen in bed with another witty, funny, sexy woman, whose apartment stood in the dark less than half a mile from ours, and instead running headlong in the other direction from her and in doing so unwittingly condemning that self to remain with an unspent erection on a stool across from a well-endowed apparition for close to a decade. My mother, it should be said, was less than twenty-five at the time. There are many ways to give oneself blue balls and this is one of them.

That newly married version of myself was only twenty-one, and my wife, to whom I ran, twenty-two. She found me out of breath and when she did, like my mother all those years before, after I explained to her that I'd run when left alone with our mutual friend of the majestic breasts, she doubled over in laughter and, without quite realizing why, or rather without admitting that I realized why, I found this laughter offensive. You were never going to do anything, she said. Of course not, I said, that's why I ran down the hill. As I said this I felt relieved both because she believed me and because I believed myself. At the same time I felt a flicker of hatred in my chest. Part of that hatred was directed at her: she knew I was too scared to do shit, so I did not do shit, and this gave her a kind of power over me, just as at the same time it provided her a measure of assurance. While it was true that I *wanted* to assure her, on some level I knew that the real reason I ran down that hill was not out of an abundance of virtue but rather out of an abundance of fear—in this case virtue and fear amounted to the same thing. In the end I directed most of this strange hatred at myself—it was both a hot and cold feeling, and might more accurately be called shame—both because blaming myself for it was easier for me to handle and because I was too confused, wittingly and unwittingly, to actually parse out what these feelings were. The fear, or so I said to myself, was not fear, it was love. Yes, I said to myself, it was love of my wife and respect of the terms of the bond we'd established with each other through getting married only a few months before that night. At the same time—or so I wanted to ask myself without allowing myself to ask myself—what on earth could cause a healthy young man to *flee* a perfectly innocent encounter at a bar with a healthy young woman? Knowledge, perhaps, that there was no such thing as innocence. All one had to do to lose one's innocence, or one's *purity* as I'd so often heard it called, was to think dirty thoughts, and, if one was exclusively attracted to women, as I thought I was, particularly large-breasted ones, as I certainly was, one only had to glimpse the aforementioned entities, even safely ensconced behind the fabric of a loose cotton T-shirt, in order to think dirty thoughts. I understood, too, that fear cannot be love and love cannot be fear. But I was not ready to allow myself to understand I understood this. If I admitted it, or so I did not then allow myself to say to myself, then even my relationship to God, who *was* love, or so I'd been told, was not made of love, which I'd been told my whole life formed the very basis of the construction of that relationship, but of fear. By that token certain aspects of my relationship with my wife, or rather one major aspect, was also constructed not from love but fear. I did not want to live this way and knew it but I also was in possession of a very powerful tool for not allowing myself to know what I knew and that was my faith. In writing this I realize I had no better luck abandoning myself there in the bar than my father's father did in building and then abandoning his fence. Repressed desire rots in the heart. Even rusted the fence remained.

One evening in the park earlier this summer, after we moved to the city where we live now, Nashville, an eight hour drive to the east of where I now sit writing these words beneath the pines in the last light of dusk, Elle and I saw a woman clad in dark leather pants that shone like the skin of a seal and were just as tight. We both agreed that she looked incredible. I asked Elle if she would ever wear a pair of pants like that. Never, she said. I said that if I were a woman I'd definitely want a pair just like them. She said: You probably would. Those pants say *look*, I said, and we both looked, didn't we? Elle agreed: she'd looked, too. And then we agreed that we both *liked* looking, and we both liked what we looked at, clad as it was in those shiny leather pants. Elle said how strange it was that we could talk about something like this now, considering everything that had happened between us earlier in the year, how strange it was that both she and I looked at the woman wearing the pants that shone like the skin of a seal and that we could together admit, now, both *that* each of us looked and that we both liked what we saw *when* we looked. There passed a silent moment in which *everything that had happened between us earlier in the year* choked the air between us. An abyss existed in that phrase, a chasm capable of carrying us, if only for a moment, back to the ashen border of the nightmare we'd endured from mid-February to early April, those months when we left the house solely to buy groceries, wiping down each and every package with dish soap and rubbing alcohol, the volcanic silence between us broken only by the running tap and the useless motion of the rag. Nothing could make us safe from each other. In the backyard, as our three-year-old son played with his toy cars only a few feet away, she and I hung by the ends of our fingers as if from the rim of a crater, each of us daring the other: You let go first. We both gave a nervous laugh. In the park below us women and men and children walked, giving each other a wide berth in the last golden light of the summer day. Scatter my ashes, my uncle said, my papa told me, and so I wrote in the first paragraph of this account, on the night of the twenty-second of November, seven months after we crawled back up onto the rocky outcropping above that crater and left that city where neither of us could any longer bear our lives together.

This, here, in the park, was better, I said. The moment passed. It was definitely better to be able to talk about it, because even if we didn't talk about it, we still thought about it. She said: Yes. One advantage women have over men, I said, is that they can wear explicitly sexual clothing in public, which means they can *be* explicitly sexual beings in public. A man can't declare himself a sexual being in such a way, or so I said to Elle while we sat in the park, because our society both takes this for granted *and,* unless the man is gay, assumes that any explicit declaration of same is tantamount to an act of sexual aggression. I do not want to make a declaration of sexual aggression, I said, lighting a cigarette there in the park, but rather to be seen just as we saw that woman: as a sexual object. You wouldn't say that, Elle said, lighting a cigarette of her own, if you were a woman yourself. It's too much pressure. What if the woman in the pants wanted to be some*one,* she said, and not some*thing*? She could wear other pants, I said. There are lots of other kinds of pants. Other kinds of pants that do not say *look at my ass*. And wouldn't it be marvelous for a moment, or so I said to Elle there in the park, not to be some*one,* but rather to be some*thing*? Maybe that was precisely what attracted me to the idea, I said. Those pants represented a chance to *have* a sexuality, rather than just wearing clothes. Elle said: Wearing clothes *is* terrible, I'll give you that. She said that if she could go totally naked right here in the park, she would. She would take off all her clothes *right now*. I said: But you wouldn't wear those pants, here in the park? Not in a million years, she said. The pants, or so she implied, continuing, were an expression of morality, whereas the body on its own expressed nothing except one's own humanity—even if one's nudity contained an explicit suggestion of sexuality, or rather, from a pragmatic perspective, made one's sexuality more readily available. The point is, she said: my body is my body. It isn't sinful on its own. Those pants are sinful, so to speak. That's why you want them. You want to be looked at, Elle said, trying and failing to stub out her cigarette in the grass, in the same way that you yourself want to look. Sure, I said: after a lifetime of being terrified of falling into temptation I think I'd like to cause *someone else* to stumble. A moment later I tripped over a small stone, which to my horror I realized was somebody's headstone, one of the many in this cemetery which were so eroded as to no longer bear a legible name. I mumbled the word sorry, still with no idea where I'd want to be buried, if I was indeed to ever be buried here, thinking of the image of my uncle's ashes, and stepped up to the cemetery's highest point, near the grave of a second- or third-cousin, adopted, who shot himself with his father's shotgun eight years ago at the age of fifteen. As I did I heard five gunshots one after the other, the pop-pop-popping pop-pop obviously discharged from a semi-automatic rifle of a smallish caliber, like a .223. I smiled: one only shoots that many times when one misses one's target. I knew this because I'd tried it, shooting at an eight-point buck with my rifle resting on my father's shoulder—or rather not quite resting—missing all three shots. Well, she said, finally succeeding in extinguishing her smoke, when you're a woman we'll have to get you a pair just like hers. You can wear them every day.

Where, I kept wondering, and kept not being able to decide,

would I want it to be, if here? My least favorite corner, or so I said to myself while I stood there, was this one, where I was standing when I heard the aforementioned five shots. The graves in that corner, where the body of the boy of fifteen lies buried, with a dark stand of pines planted by a forestry company rising on the other side of the fence, received the least light of any in the whole cemetery. By my count, or so I reckoned them up as I walked there, at least four people had committed suicide in this community in the last decade or so, two of them teenage boys, the other two middle-aged men in advanced states of estrangement from their families. Two men in their twenties had been murdered. Only three hundred or so people called this place their home, or perhaps in the neighborhood of four hundred if one counted the more solitary and often transient members of the population set back in the surrounding woods and thick brush crowding in amongst these high hills and low creek bottoms. When I was a boy my mother often rented VHS tapes for me at a gas station with a giant sawmill blade affixed to its side. This store was called the Rough Cut, and the man who owned it often gave me candy. His name was Floyd. When I was seven or eight he was murdered by a man who lived only a few miles over the other side of the state line, a mechanic to whose garage my father's father had taken me only a year or two earlier for repairs on his pickup, a memory I suspect I have retained only because there stood, in the garage, a Pac-Man machine that had been wired to work without quarters on which I played while my father's father conferred with the mechanic about his pickup. It was most likely during the week that followed Floyd's death that I heard the story told of how Floyd had been carrying on—this was the accepted phrase in the community—with the mechanic's wife. The mechanic had already given him a warning. If he ever saw him with his wife again, he said, or so the story went, he would kill him. Evidently Floyd was not dissuaded by this warning, which might now more accurately be described as a guarantee. One day he crossed the state line and drove up to the mechanic's house with the mechanic's wife and kids with him, and the mechanic, who saw them drive up, went into his house, came out with a gun, and shot Floyd dead there in the driver's seat of his car with the man's own wife and kids still sitting in it—or so I recall the story as it was told to me when I was a boy. DON'T COME IN HERE, my mother said.

Throughout most of my childhood my best friend lived a few miles up the mountain from the Rough Cut. At his fourteenth or fifteenth birthday party we went swimming in the creek that ran cold and clear in the ravine below his house. There were five of us boys, all the others older than me save one. We'd all known each other since we were small. It was warm for March but the creek, which emerged from a spring higher up the mountain, was still ice-cold. For some reason unbeknownst to me, and likely to them as well, all of the older boys had recently taken to suddenly baring their asses in the direction of each other, usually at surprising moments, such as when one had just entered a room. That day one of the older boys jumped into the deepest part of the creek and came up without his shorts on at all. We laughed and pointed. Afterward, in the one-bedroom cabin which stood fifty or so yards from the stream that my best friend's parents had allowed us to make use of for the night, we peeled off our wet shorts to much the same laughter, which was both of a piece with and wholly different from the laughter we'd been laughing our whole childhoods together. Another day, years before, several of us had rolled a younger boy down a short incline into a puddle.

We laughed as we rolled him and the boy laughed as he rolled. I'm not doing that again, my father said after I fired my three shots one-after-the-other with the semi-automatic .223, missing the buck on the barren hillside above. I felt the bullets whistle past my ear, he said. The boy was four. I was six.

Those pines beyond the cemetery are only ten or twelve years old at most—at least a full three decades younger than the ones that stand beyond the pond. Standing next to the fifteen-year-old's grave I wondered how long it would be before they cut them down again. Five years? Eight? Since my last writing I have traveled back to Tennessee, where all my life before moving here I said I would never live, because it's part of the South, an assertion I first inwardly made after encountering a book about Jim Crow during a family vacation to Mississippi to visit the Vicksburg battlefield, the book's pages filled with black-and-white photographs of black bodies bound and hanged and shot, many of them burnt, each without exception surrounded by smiling white Southerners who looked as happy as if in attendance at a Fourth of July barbecue—I read the phrase *it was open season on blacks* and thought with horror of the deer we shot and gutted and skinned every fall—and there, in the back of the car, I swore I would never live here, not in Mississippi, not in the South, and cannot recall ever having been so relieved to be back in Oklahoma. Because I did not consider myself, nor my home state, to be Southern, it never occurred to me that such lynchings also might have happened there as well. I'd never heard myself speak from outside my own head and could not then hear the unmistakable accent passed down to me, nor make out the unelucidated history expressed in the sound of my own voice. Last night on the porch of my father's house I waited with him for my sister to arrive from the city where she lives four hours southeast of here, which was quite spectacularly burned to the ground in the November of 1864, Atlanta, which she was leaving for the purpose of celebrating with us the national holiday first officially declared as annual immediately upon the burning of that city, and as such was not intended to be a holiday held in *memoria* of that famous dinner held by the Pilgrims and the Native Americans whom they would shortly slaughter but rather a celebration of the total destruction of Atlanta. My father told me several hunting stories while we smoked and waited. The stories came one after the other, each leading into the next after a brief pause for my reaction to the story just told. As usual I told no stories and this, as it often does, resulted in some discomfort on my part, for I wished to take part in a more than passive sense, but I couldn't, because nearly every hunting story I have was already known to my father because he was there with me when the material which later became my own hunting story took place. Of course I have already heard nearly all of his hunting stories, too, but this does not matter, because it is a father's privilege to repeat himself to his son while the reverse is not the case. After writing the initial version of several of the immediately preceding paragraphs by the pond at dusk, I walked into the greater darkness of the pines, taking a trail I have walked many times before, though seldom from the direction I now took. The path from where I joined it heads northwest and then straight west through the pines, then north, where it enters the old deciduous woods that still line the river, live oak and elm and massive first-growth beech trees, the undergrowth thick with greenbrier and grapevine, travelling in a west-east motion along the river bank. It was the army of William Tecumseh Sherman that burned the city where my sister lives, igniting that citywide conflagration toward the end of that war in which I myself fought and was killed numerous times in this very river bottom, though, in harmony with my then-belief in the ultimate resurrection of the body, I rose again each time to fight anew, wearing the blue kepi cap my father had bought me when I was six or seven. (It was partly my own daily participation in that so-called war between the states that led to my interest in the history of its aftermath, which in turn led to the oath, now broken, never to move to the South.) My father was now telling the story of the best cigar he'd ever smoked, at daybreak one morning while turkey hunting. In the story he was in the deep woods at first light, crouched under the pines, listening to two different turkeys gobble in the shadows of the hills on either side of him; he lights the cigar and listens to them, feeling the particular sensation of truly being alive which is perhaps best afforded through the use of tobacco at daybreak. He is fond of this story and so am I, but, somewhat spooked by the swiftly falling darkness, I hurried my steps along the riverbank until I came to the precise spot where I have long intended one day to kill myself. I stopped there and lit a cigarette.

Though I could not last night think of a story to tell my father, one comes to me now, of a day spent on the humid and windy shore of the Gulf of Mexico, recalled from around the same time as the day at the creek when the boy emerged from the water sans pants, locked within me until now, writing this: in the roofless public shower with my cousin, four years older than me, the amber late afternoon light and the sandy smell of the beach and the brackish water of the nearby slough over which we'd walked on creaking boards, the slough's ochre appearance oddly suggestive to me of wickedness, perhaps brought on by the sign-warned presence of alligators, waves from the gulf crashing in the distance, the shower's purpose, ostensibly, to soap off the sand of that muddy water, my cousin standing a few feet away with his back turned, and my erection, stone-hard, which would not, for all I inwardly said to it, subside. And why? I did not know then what my body with silent blood-filled force was saying to me about myself, possessed no words for the experience itself or what it meant, he and I there in the shower alone, the strange buzz I felt in the one moment he turned and saw me in that state, and me thinking—hoping—both then and immediately afterward that perhaps it (I, the erection) was normal. I shelved the memory that day, without knowing why, seldom ever again to take it down and, like a forbidden text, open it to that salt-filled page. That I never finished public school—home-schooled from thirteen on—and so never again showered with other boys saved me perhaps from a kind of knowledge that would not come until far later, on a nude beach on the south Florida coast, watching a queer boy chat with a trans girl, her huge penis hanging beneath her wrapped breasts, my own member rising with the twink's as he spoke to her: there it was. Desire never named and only half-suspected, suddenly and fully present, without a word. All denial there: ended. Next to Elle—there with me the whole time, asleep, both of us as naked as the trans girl and the queer boy who stood thirty yards away from us with their feet in the soughing green surf—I laughed with astonishment, and said goodbye to a version of myself whom I'd thought would always be who I was, thinking, now, as I write this beneath the pines near my apartment, *bi bi bi,* the misspelled titular chorus of a song my friends by the creek had performed once for a talent show in the year 2000, an act which, now that I more than two decades later recalled watching them perform it, gave name to that same strange feeling. And why did I feel so left out in not having helped perform the song, if not in part for having failed to *exhibit* that facet of myself, which I did not yet then know was even there? Always, before that day on the beach, naked, I thought my feeling could be credited to simply being left out. Now not so much. Can one regret what one does not know even *while* one does not know it? A strong and increasing suspicion: yes.

On the porch my father mentioned that he and his father, the man who in his madness with his son drove fenceposts into the ground all along the pine plantation that borders the hardwood forest that in turn borders the river, both men who strung barbed wire along those fenceposts with the intent never subsequently realized to eventually run cows on the land, spent many a happy hour, my father said, shooting hundreds of rounds into the backs of turtles from his father's father's balcony, which hangs high up on the bluff above the river to the east of where I now stood smoking in the place where I long ago determined I would one day end my life. My father mentioned this as if he did not expect me to remember this story, but I said that I not only remembered it but in fact recalled having participated. My uncle his sister's husband was there, along with my cousin, and my father's father's brother. I remember taking a turn with the short Remington .22 that already belonged to me even at age seven, finding a turtle in my scope in the shallows below. The turtle's shell burst with the shot, flooding the water around it with blood. I pulled back the bolt, discharged the hot shell, added another cartridge into the chamber, clacked it shut—that sound, as with all sounds involving the chambering or ejecting of a cartridge, still exerts a oneiric power over my imagination—then brought the scope back to my eye and searched in it for another turtle. The opposite side of the river from where I stood on the path rose steeply above the water, mostly pines climbing the hillside's rocky soil. The time of day was what is commonly called the blue hour, but the many leaves that had fallen in the past few weeks had turned the hillside beneath the pines, which there intermix with hardwoods, into a deep and luxuriant red. The river's surface reflected a dull gray, though I knew the water itself to be clear. Not long after Floyd's death someone took—or stole—the giant blade. The building still stands, though the door has hung askew on one hinge now for nigh on two decades. Weeds have grown up alongside the abandoned pumps. After the funerals of various family members I have noticed his headstone, taller than most of the others in the secluded cemetery in which it stands, four or five hundred yards through the woods from the church I attended from one end to the other of my childhood, about the same distance from the little schoolhouse in which my mother attended kindergarten and elementary school, long since consolidated, which is another way of saying shut down and abandoned. I cannot now remember Floyd's last name. I think he may have shared it with my mother and her father and brother, though there was no relation that I know of between my maternal relatives and the man who owned the Rough Cut and was shot dead just on the other side of the state line. My sister's car pulled onto the street in front of my father's house. Hey brother, she said as she got out, pronouncing it as she always does on first seeing me, as in *bother*.

Over the years I have returned to this spot by the river on a number of occasions to contemplate the action I intended and still intend, as of the initial writing of this sentence, one day to undertake there, where the river runs east-to-west before making a sharp turn down to my left at the foot of the bluff above which my father thirteen years ago attempted to construct a lodge, which burned one night in a fierce blaze shortly before its completion. For many years—the years during which I picked this spot in which to die—the site on the bluff above the river's lower elbow sat empty, the burned remains of the would-be lodge like the empty socket left behind by a pulled tooth, the site itself mostly charred timbers and melted glass. A few years ago my father sold the site, and a rich man and his wife constructed a massive house in the exact place where the former building burned. Now when I stand in this spot in my body and contemplate the death of my body, which was always before a simultaneous contemplation of the river, I feel the house of the rich man and his wife looking down on me, on top of the bluff which makes the river turn. The spell is broken. Now when I stand there I press very close to an oak on my left which blocks the mansion from view and I stare straight at the river and the hillside rising above it. This time I smoked and, instead of contemplating my future final moments, stood there inwardly complaining about the ugly house of the rich man and his wife and watched as the lack of light turned the opposite hillside's redness a dirty shade of brown, while the river became the color of too many paints mixed together. In my mind I imagined not the would-be lodge burning but rather the house of the rich man and his wife. Hey sister, I said, pronouncing it as I always do on first seeing her, as in *Easter*. I turned to go.

In the time I've been writing the above here in the city in the South where I live, the sun has gone down behind the three pines that stand seventy yards or so from where I sit writing. Their highest boughs reach up black against the pale darkening sky. The middle pine stands the tallest. The uppermost boughs have prominent branches that reach out in each direction like arms, while all three also possess distinctly headlike top branches, reaching directly into the sky. Taken together while writing these words the three pines brought to my mind a collection of crosses such as one sees sometimes dotting the landscape of the rural South, often but not always near churches, their number evoking not only Christ and the two thieves, the one he said would be with him in heaven and the one who scoffed at him, urging Christ to prove that he was the son of God, but also the three members of the Holy Trinity. (It strikes me that I have never thought of this association before: that the three crosses stand not only for the three crucified that day on Golgotha, in that thirty-fourth year of our age, but also for the Trinity itself. But which of its members could be said to be the Savior? Which the thieves?) I walked along the riverbank until I came to the place where the path leads up toward the house of my childhood. It was almost full dark by the time I ascended the short lip (the site of many Civil War battles fought there, all unnamed) and into the trees that border the yard, past the holly beneath which lies one part of the buried ashes of a beloved dog (the rest of the dog's ashes I scattered in the river, while my wife and sister and father stood behind me: some sank, some floated away). I saw the lights of the house a hundred yards ahead and heard the voices of my son and Elle on the back porch, and it occurred to me as I stepped toward them and the house that almost exactly two years before I had stood smoking on the side porch of that same house at dusk just before Thanksgiving dinner and saw a form that resembled my father coming up out of the river bottom at the same exact time of day as I was now approaching the house, and that that fatherlike figure had at first not appeared to be my father at all, but rather an apparition or ghost of him, approaching in the advancing dusk, until that moment when, only twenty or so yards away, the wavering form at last resumed his sturdy likeness, and said my name in greeting.

I have had for almost two full years now in my head an entity whom I first met when she appeared in a novel I was then writing. The first thing she did upon entering the novel was have sex with its protagonist, surprising both character and writer with her sudden desire, and I have long thought, in these two years she's been with me both in my head and on the page, that I too would have liked to have her move upon me in such a way. She resembles a famous French actress now in her late sixties in every physical detail, and this is how she first appeared to me, as a both overtly intelligent and sexual creature, which is more or less what I have wished myself to be, though I, never having worn any such pants as those mentioned in the pages above, have for the greater duration of my life endeavored toward the former while denying the latter. Even though she is part of my own mind, or was before I placed her there on the page, she is smarter by far than I am, and a better writer, by which I mean to say that she has often said things which I did not myself understand, which later seemed to me far more intelligent than anything I could have thought or imagined on my own. It is probably not worth remarking that this may be an aspect of my own vanity. Nor do I mean to imply that she wrote the words herself but rather that this character seems to have had access to things about both herself and myself to which I do not myself have access. This is a common enough realization on its own for a writer to come to about one of his characters, so much so that some better word than realization ought to be used. What interests me here, rather, is the sexual desire that I immediately felt for the character, who is not me, though certainly a product of me or of my mind, which is one part of the entity (not entities) that I generally consider to be myself.

My sexual desire for the character does not seem to me a sexual desire for myself but rather for another person, who exists nowhere but in my own mind. But that is not quite right. She exists now as an entity in the novel she first appeared in. She would not exist even in my mind if she had not first appeared on the page I was then writing. (This, then, is lust for a fiction—I'd wager: always the case. Without fiction, no desire.) Since I stopped writing the novel I have missed her, both as an object of desire and as an intelligence greater than my own—far more for the second characteristic than for the first. When I first showed a draft of this manuscript to my friend who is a poet, he commented on this woman's status as an object of sexual desire in the book. He felt that I had shortchanged her and that she had more to say. My literary agent at the time also said that she wanted to know more about the woman's story. These comments taken together aligned with an intuition I seemed to have come to independently of both agent and poet-friend, which was that this character formed in some way the novel's invigorating spirit, and when I revised the work she made it known that this was the truth, and even that she was irritated with me for having allowed her in the earlier draft to say so little of what she wanted to say. Given room to step forth from her status as object—and as fiction—she spoke the thing not only that she wanted to say, but which the novel itself had wanted to speak into being, and she did this quite on her own, for I did not know what she was going to say when she said the thing that was quite rightly, or so I thought, what the novel itself wanted to say, for what the novel had lacked up to that point was to be allowed to speak for itself rather than I through it. The thing she said—and which I still do not completely understand—was that a novel must be written in two languages. First in the one the author knows, and then in a language the author does not know. This second language is most important, or so she said, for it is in this unknown language that the novel itself speaks independently of its author. I will not extrapolate here on whether this is the reason I found or find her attractive in an erotic sense. It seems to me natural enough, if also risible, that the writing mind occasionally creates sexualized versions of characters to whom the writer is him- or herself erotically attracted. After all, the mind which produces the fiction is as much a part of the body as are the genitals. Even the greatest of painters have often not regarded themselves as being above drawing their own pornography. In certain instances this pornographic impulse has likely led to more interesting work than in the artists' actual creations or so-called actual *masterworks*. Many painters have made very fruitful careers for themselves by refusing to distinguish the two at all. It simply does not read as well in the catalogues of the gallerists and auctioneers, or in the minds, if they can indeed be said to have them, of the filthy rich who buy the paintings and the hordes of so-called art-appreciators who frequent the halls of both the great and less great museums to call a painting like Edvard Munch's *Madonna* a great work of smut rather than a great work of art. And yet the one fact fails to exclude the other. My own first reaction to that painting at age seventeen cannot be truthfully described as having been wholly aesthetic in nature.

When my father said my name in greeting we went into the house and there ate Thanksgiving dinner with my maternal grandfather and grandmother, my mother and son and wife. On that night I feared because of a persistent pain in my chest that this would be the final Thanksgiving for which I would be physically present, and tried to distract myself by making video recordings of my family members, which had the unintended consequence of giving me the unmistakable sensation that I was already not there in the flesh, but rather had already taken on the form and substance of a ghost, no more alive than that girl in the oil painting mentioned in the pages above. The second anniversary of that night is tomorrow, the twenty-first Thanksgiving of the new millennium, one hundred and fifty-seven years since that most notable declaration of that holiday in this country, celebrating the total reduction of a Southern city to smoke and ash, and 1,987 years since the death by blood loss and ultimately asphyxiation while nailed to a piece of wood of the man by whose birth we mark the beginning of the present epoch. The character for whom I feel this present sexual attraction will tomorrow be almost two years old in terms of her life in my mind while on the page she remains in her mid-sixties, the moment I ran down the hill from the young woman at the bar will have taken place just over nine years ago, and it will have been twenty-six or twenty-seven years since the day I saw my mother naked in her closet at the Fears cabin. One cannot fail to enter a room in which one already stands. Atlanta had it coming.

Yesterday, before beginning to write, because I had spent too much time on the internet, specifically on social media, I felt it would be impossible to get my being to occupy the necessary form in which to write. I got up from the wrought-iron table on the patio where I normally work and went inside my apartment, where I took down my copy of *Ulysses* and opened it at random, hoping that the rhythm of the language contained in that work would provide a cleansing effect. Intending to quote from that same section I read yesterday I brought out with me to write today what I thought was *Ulysses* but actually proved on closer inspection to be the H.T. Lowe-Porter translation of *The Magic Mountain*, my copy of which has a similar binding and red cover as that of the former novel, though the Lowe-Porter translation is of a reddish-orange hue, rather than the brighter scarlet of the book composed, or so its author claimed, in Trieste–Zürich–Paris from 1914–1921. Opening the reddish-orange copy at random my eye first fell on "Christmas! Hans Castorp had never once thought of it." Turning at random again I found: "To speak of sorrow would be disingenuous." Three days ago, on the twenty-third day of this month, I climbed onto the four-wheeler my father keeps in a shed near the house where I grew up and drove through the gold-tinted afternoon sunlight and cold shadows about three miles by dirt road and blacktop to the cemetery where I hope, or so I've two or three times written in the pages above, or at least enough times to have begun to doubt the legitimacy of said claim, to one day have a headstone with my name on it. While I was walking among the graves there, coming first as is my habit to the grave of my maternal grandmother's parents, I heard the sounds of small voices and was momentarily startled, anxious about what would happen if I was seen to be there in the cemetery alone, as if I had no right to be there near the grave of my grandmother's parents. The voices belonged to two boys. They'd walked up from the house nearest the cemetery, which stands on the other side of a shallow ravine three or four hundred yards away from the headstones, likely having heard the sound of my four-wheeler, curious. Too far away for me to make out their faces, they looked through the fence and then headed back in the direction from which they came. I was relieved they had not attempted to speak with me. It now occurs to me, writing this, as it no doubt occurred to me (without occurring to me) while I was walking there, that it always gives me pleasure when at this cemetery to look at the oldest headstones, many of them so worn down they no longer bear the names of the bodies whose graves they still mark, such as the one I mentioned tripping over some pages ago. Most of the oldest legible remaining stones tilting or listing above the graves bear the names of some of the cemetery's youngest occupants. In the oldest part of the cemetery stands a great oak, and beneath this tree are buried a boy who lived twenty days in 1925, and a boy with the same last name (his older brother, perhaps) who ten years earlier lived only one year and three months, or 462 days, to which figure I have just now arrived with the assistance of my computer calculator. Next to those boys lies a young girl who bore the same last name as my maternal grandmother's maiden name, born on 8 October 1914 and dead 30 April 1917. GONE HOME. A few steps from the dead boys and girl lies a joint mother-daughter grave, both lives ended in 1955. The mother was thirty-two, the daughter eight. Near them lay the grave of a girl who also bore the same last name as my mother's mother's parents, dead at two in 1922. A girl of thirteen dead in 1926 lies next to a boy with the same last name dead at eight in 1928. A boy with my mother's maiden name—these distant dead relatives of mine lie everywhere here—dead at eight, his grave entirely covered with plastic flowers, a living wild rose bush, and a Lego set. He was buried July of last year. Beside the boy's grave stands a bench with a wooden seat and cast-iron seatback in which were wrought the words WE LOVED HIM A LOT BUT GOD LOVED HIM MORE. This is near the southwest corner of the cemetery, just beneath its highest point, fifty feet or so from the boy my second or third cousin, adopted, who shot himself eight years ago because he was afraid of the punishment, or so I heard it said, that he feared his father would mete out upon him when he arrived home later that night, because the boy, fifteen, had been riding his father's four-wheeler without permission. I was walking away from that grave when I heard the five gunshots in quick succession and smiled.

Now, and during the initial writing of the above paragraph, it is Thanksgiving day, gray as I have always preferred this holiday to be ever since I was a little boy. I remember one Thanksgiving that was sunny and warm, almost like spring or even early summer, and the disappointment I felt as I stood looking out the window of the dining room of my father's father's house, as if the lack of wintry weather proved the fact that our Thanksgiving was not the real thing, that, no matter how we tried, it would not really be the holiday itself, but rather a shoddy imitation of the real thing, celebrated by real people in real places, unlike our unreal sunny holiday, as if the presence of this spring-like warmth indicated our own lack of reality as compared to everyone else's, implicitly bringing up that old feeling or fear relating to the clandestine filming of my life: other people's lives were more real than mine, and as such, or so I thought, must make for better films. I say *initial writing* here and elsewhere in this writing because I seldom if ever leave a paragraph alone after I've written it. The author of *Ulysses* drafted parts of that book with red and green and blue crayons, a fact which has not once ceased to delight me ever since I years ago learned it. I do most of my writing with the ends of my fingers and try not to get cigarette ashes in the keyboard. It must be said, though it is perhaps not worth remarking on, that I do not usually succeed in the endeavor.

The last grave of which I took note before leaving the cemetery belonged to a girl who lived just six days in 1964, three years after the birth of my father and five before the birth of my mother, who was born in the same former tuberculosis sanatorium or asylum in which she would, just over two decades after being born herself, later give birth to me, in a grim-looking stone building on the other side of the mountains from the town, if it could actually be called a town, in which she'd grown up and where she would later raise me. The former sanatorium and hospital, located a few miles outside a town called Talihina (*tal-ih-hee-nuh*, a combination of two Choctaw words meaning *iron road*), is now surrounded by tall barbed wire fences and signs saying GOVERNMENT PROPERTY and KEEP OUT, the grounds encompassed by some of the tallest pines I've ever seen in that part of the state, standing half a mile or so off the highway where, late one summer night a few years before I was born, in the same year that his mother and best friend both died, while my father's father and my father's mother were headed home from fishing at Lake Sardis and thus towing a bass boat, an eighteen-year-old drunk driver in a pickup truck headed in the opposite direction crossed the center line. My grandfather swerved to miss him, but the sudden motion caused the boat he was pulling to jackknife. The boat crashed through the cab of the oncoming pickup. My grandfather saw the boy's brain spattered on the road. He found what was left of his head in the ditch. It strikes me that the horror of that night very likely returned to him even the day he came to see me for the first time, the newborn son of his only son, passing by the site of the wreck on the way to the hospital. Some years later, at the edge of a particular darkness of pines, he and my father stretched barbed-wire from post to post, erecting a fence in order to try to help him fix his mind. And then, after his death, the only son of his only son sat down at a particular wrought-iron table in Tennessee to write, not thinking at all about the events of that awful night until the writing turned in the direction of the former sanatorium, itself surrounded by barbed-wire, and, upon reaching a certain spot on the darkened highway near the now barricaded and abandoned building, that only son of an only son, as if for a moment buried in that darkness both with the dead boy and the dead man who killed him, slowly began to bring together the words of this paragraph.

I have just read somewhere or other, either yesterday or earlier today, that the word *tuberculosis* is never once used in *The Magic Mountain*, a novel Thomas Mann began writing in 1912 and which ultimately took him twelve years to complete. I do not speak German and therefore cannot verify this claim; the word is used over and over in the translation I've been reading. For some reason I *do* know that Thomas Mann smoked exactly twelve cigarettes a day, allowing himself the further luxury of two diurnal cigars, and I also know that he confessed in the privacy of his diary that he felt a desire for his young son when he glimpsed him in the bath, and that this desire both disquieted and disturbed him. In the time so far that I have been writing the initial version of this paragraph and the preceding one today, I have smoked eight cigarettes and have a ninth sticking out of my mouth. I do not usually count them and am loath to count anything else. Once, when I was nine or ten, on either Thanksgiving or Christmas Eve, my mother sent me with her brother to help him feed his cows. He drank beer after beer pulled from a small ice chest he kept in the back of his truck. I asked him what it tasted like. Bubbly water I guess, he said. I knew drinking while driving was illegal, but I'd also never seen anyone do it, let alone been in a moving vehicle with someone who was doing it. The beer seemed to have no effect whatsoever on him. He said nothing and I said nothing and only when I asked him about the beer did he seem slightly startled, as if he had not expected me to notice or had not even noticed himself that he was drinking. (Three or four beers, I think it was: these to me seemed like a million.) Though it is only half-past two in the afternoon the sun is already going down through the high outstretched oaks that stand to the southwest of my patio. The three pines about which I yesterday wrote stand to the west of the oaks. The one furthest to the right is almost black, while the two to its right, closer to the increasingly acute angle of sunlight, are blackish-green and in the boughs more illuminated forest-green. Though I seldom leave a paragraph alone after I've written it, I have a persistent fantasy of doing so, like a few of the writers of whom I've heard, who claim to leave all their writing as it initially appears, the flagrant irresponsibility of which I find attractive, though not in the same way I find attractive the writer-character in my head who is more intelligent than I am. Flagrant: I like the extravagance of the word, both in the sense of its relation to *conflagration* and *in flagrante delicto* and *enfilade* fire, the act of many men standing shoulder-to-shoulder all firing their rifles at once, as soldiers on both sides of our war did into columns of advancing men, in some cases filling the air with so many Minié balls as to make the air gray with lead. What, I wonder, did he think of, standing there in the ditch? What could he possibly have said to the remains of that boy, smeared there all over the road? What could he possibly have said to himself?

My father has told me that on the few occasions—perhaps the *only* occasion—on which they talked about that night, his mother my grandmother vehemently pointed out that the boy had been drunk, as if, my father said, the mere fact of the dead boy's drunkenness somehow made things better, more explicable, somehow less horrible, when of course nothing could make it less horrible because nothing could rewind time, or so I now think, revising these paragraphs: no matter how much better it felt to say that he was the one at fault, he was the one who was drunk, he was the one who crossed the center line, there was no revision to be made of that night, no way of cleansing the surface of that dark road, because either way, the boat did what it did to his head. He wasn't drunk anymore. He wasn't ever getting drunk again. The poet John Berryman, who drank himself as close to oblivion as he could nearly every day for the better part of the final two decades of his life, and who frequently made inebriated attempts at the seduction of his friends' wives, secretly worrying all the while that he was a homosexual—while at college he once wrote to a friend that he had received his letter *with prick pricked*—smoked on average three-to-five packs of cigarettes, which is to say somewhere between sixty and a hundred smokes. For my part I average between a more modest twenty-five and forty. By even a conservative estimate—call it thirty a day—I have smoked around ten thousand cigarettes in the past year. In his interview with *The Paris Review*, Berryman said that the day he visited W.B. Yeats, in April or May of 1937, Yeats, then well-advanced in age, told the young poet—a mere twenty-two—that he only ever revised anymore in the interest of a more passionate syntax, which statement Berryman said puzzled him then, and still puzzled him now that he himself was a self-described old man. Berryman was only in his mid-fifties when he declared himself old. He was correct in the assessment, however, as he died in 1972 at the age of fifty-seven having leapt from a high bridge over the Mississippi River, into which the river that runs behind my childhood home eventually flows by way of other and more famous rivers. When Berryman leapt he did not hit the river but rather smacked the frozen mud on the bank.

I once attempted to figure out the actual speed of his fall—to the best of my rough calculations, forty-five miles per hour. Today I have written in the neighborhood of fourteen hundred words and for now am finished. The afternoon is getting on and the Thanksgiving day sun has almost gone down over the wall that hems in the patio where I have been writing the initial version of this paragraph. My hands are cold. The Minié ball, or so I have just read via the assistance of an internet search engine, traveled at a rate of nearly six *hundred* miles per hour. I have not failed to notice a growing preponderance of numerical figures in this document, but thus far I have failed to grasp their significance, if any.

When I was young I was taught by the church to believe that I deserved destruction. They called the doctrine original sin and said it required hell from the very first sinful breath—only to be alleviated by the death of the son, his resurrection, and one's belief in same. Of all I was taught within the four walls of that institution with its spearlike and sky-pointed phallus and the great iron bell the adults rang to call us kids in from play to learn about the evil hidden within each and every one of us, this belief in deserved damnation seems to be the only one to have remained. We learned this in a room called the *sanctuary*. The speed limit of that stretch of road near the former sanatorium or asylum—another word, it now occurs to me, for *sanctuary*—is, if I recall correctly, fifty-five miles per hour. I do not know how fast my grandfather was going nor the speed of the boy who died there.

In writing this, without quite knowing why, I want to know who washed the blood off the bow of the boat. But who else would it have been? I see him standing in his driveway next to the garage with the hose. I see him sweating there next to the garage with the hose in one hand and the other hanging empty at his side. He is alone. It is just him and his sweat and the boat and the blood and the woods beyond and the idiot birds ceaselessly calling to each other in the trees. The woods are never quiet here but he is quiet in them and he is alone, standing there sweating with the hose in the heat. I want to reach out and take his empty hand. I want to reach out and take his empty hand, but I can't. It's not that I want to undo what happened that night. There is no undoing any horror in this world or any other. Knowing this, I cannot quite account for the thing that happens to the image: as he stands there in my mind and now on this page next to the boat and its blood, in that moment, in his despair, thinking about the boy he killed, he himself becomes a boy again, the same boy I have seen in a certain photograph I have of him when he was ten years old, a portrait of an Okie boy in overalls, his gaze open and direct at the camera. Even those eyes, the boy's eyes, the eyes of my father's father, the glimpse of which I sometimes catch in the gaze of my own son, look enflamed, as if the world within him already burns like a city in the dark. The boy in the photograph who now stands by the bloody boat looks for all the world like he knows everything that will come to pass, seeing it even as he cannot see it: his future and its darkness; a future utterly without sanctuary, with no hand to grasp but his own.

One fails to grasp the significance of one's writing by necessity. This failure enables further writing. Anything understood cannot be written. On the other hand—my grandfather's hand remains untaken—my grandfather's hand now bones in a box in a grave—or so I have increasingly come to feel, we understand far more about ourselves than that of which we allow ourselves to be cognizant, and so, in a sense, that which we understand and keep secret from ourselves represents precisely that about which we ought to write. And yet writing, as with understanding, makes life worse. Art doesn't save lives. It ruins them. Most artists' biographies bear out precisely this point. The relentless contemplation of the self required in order to make art or even engage with it on a serious level is frequently destructive of the very will to continue to be oneself, which is why those who undertake a life of reading are infinitely more guilt-ridden, morose, and prone to bouts of absolute despair than those who don't, why poets jump off bridges and stick their heads in ovens and why writers drink and why novelists like me fail to do their laundry and instead lie around all day naked in bed while most people, which is to say those that don't write or read, spend the greater portion of their lives studiously avoiding doing anything which might draw them into contact with themselves, such as aesthetically or intellectually ambitious art, and is the reason why most people hate writing to start with and writers especially and literature in general, for the very function of writing and writers and literature is to bring people into contact not with others but with *themselves,* and this contact, for most of us, is *unbearable,* because we find ourselves *unbearable,* because what we find when we find ourselves is that thing we know better than anything else about ourselves even though we hate knowing it and do not want to know it—our *pain.* When I avoid art, when I avoid reading actual books, when I avoid my own thoughts, as I often do the more depressed I become, I do so out of a desire to avoid *me,* which is a desire to avoid my pain. I am exhausted with my pain, which is why I am exhausted with myself, and the trouble with pain, or so I now think, writing this, when endured over a lengthy span of time, is that it's *monstrously* boring. There is nothing inherently interesting about pain. It just goes on and on sanding the edges off anything that might cut through the awful boredom of pain itself. It's probably not worth remarking that in the sentence immediately preceding this one where I wrote *pain* I should've written *depression,* which is nothing more than pain stretched out and endured for an indefinite period of time. The Thanksgiving day sun is gone now. I did not stop writing where, a few paragraphs ago, I said I was finished writing. Elle woke naked beside me there on that south Florida beach and I told her about the twink and his member and mine and she laughed. You just came out to me, she said, didn't you. And I had to say that I supposed that this was so. The boy was drunk, she said.

Rereading the initial version of the previous paragraph, written yesterday, my mind amended the sentence "This failure enables further writing" to "This failure ennobles further writing." When I think of the word *noble,* the first writer to come to mind is Thomas Mann. Earlier today when reading Mann on the back porch of my parents' house, both Mann—in a different translation than that mentioned earlier, this Mann bound in paper rather than cloth—and I were shat upon by a bird. I have always heard that being shat upon by a bird means good luck for the one who has been shitted upon, but it seems probable to me that this truism is merely the inverse result of how one naturally feels when another creature evacuates the contents of its bowels upon one's person, an attempt to slough off bad fortune by calling it a good omen. I also now wonder whether Mann would still be Mann if he, while writing *The Magic Mountain,* had been regularly shitted upon by birds, or if he had, instead of writing his gigantic and generally mirthless novels, instead allowed himself to submit to certain urges, such as the desire to touch the naked skin of young men—perhaps glimpsed at a beach shower nearby a salt-filled slough—rather than that of his devoted wife, or so I now wonder, writing this at

5:09pm the day after Thanksgiving, though the word *day* is not technically accurate because it is already full dark here in this city in the South, not of course because we are far north, but because we are close to the invisible line dividing the eastern time zone from the central one. This is the furthest east I have ever lived, just north and east of that state where I read in the back of the car about the *open season*. Yesterday, after I finished writing the initial versions of several of the preceding paragraphs my father and I sat on his back patio and he told me several hunting stories which I had heard previously but whose details had faded from my mind. I bring this up only to mention two facts of which he made uncharacteristically precise note. We were talking about how quickly darkness falls here. You killed your first deer at 5:35pm on the Saturday after Thanksgiving, he said. That nine point. And I killed that buck that hangs in the living room of the house the next day, on Sunday, also at 5:35pm, right at dark, he said. The author of *Ulysses*, in a letter to Nora Barnacle his wife, once wrote: "You say you will shit your drawers, dear, and let me fuck you then. I would like to hear you shit them, dear, first and then fuck you. Some night when we are somewhere in the dark and talking dirty and you feel your shit ready to fall put your arms round my neck in shame and shit it down softly..." While there are many ways to give oneself blue balls, as I mentioned above some pages ago, this may be one way of relieving them. John Berryman once wrote in a letter to a younger writer that the whole reason, or at least one of the reasons, for his incessant attempts at seducing the wives of his friends, emerged out of a desire to be close (*close!*) to them. (His *pals*, or so in late middle-age ((his old age)) he called them: of all the words we use to refer to our intimates, the most desexualized.) James Joyce wrote lovingly of Nora's farts and of wanting her to shit her drawers before she fucked him. At the moment I have nothing further to add on either account.

I realize now that I have not mentioned this buck the head of which hangs high above the living room, or rather high up within the living room, of the house of my childhood, where I was staying when I wrote the first versions of the first sentences of this account. For several years I hoped myself to kill such a deer as my father had killed on that particular Sunday, but I never managed to do so. Writing this now I am tempted to calculate how many days it has been since I killed that first one, shot with my father's .223, a semi-automatic Ruger Mini-14, right at dusk. It did not run far before we found it fallen in the dead grass. I do not know how quickly the deer, nor the birdshit that today struck both me and Thomas Mann, fell—though according to his biographers mostly skin-and-bones at the time of his death, the poet John Berryman almost certainly fell faster than either, though not as fast as a Minié ball fired during the siege and, later, the fall of that Southern city wherein lives my youngest sister, nor perhaps as fast as the boat that went through the cab of a certain pickup near a certain former sanatorium. Berryman's own father, or so I somewhere once read, I think, or at least *want* to think, was buried in the Holdenville cemetery, mentioned earlier in these pages as being located in that county where my father and his father were born. I do not know where the boy who died that night is buried. I do not even know his name. Berryman, future poet, a boy of eleven on the day of his father's death by self-administered gunshot, the boy who as a man would, only a few years before himself leaping from that bridge, write: *The marker slants, flowerless, day's almost done*—wondering, as he did, *when will indifference come*. But it did not come.

It did not come. He never saw his father's grave himself: as such, the scene in the poem and its slanted marker: a fiction. No one bearing my own last name lies buried in the cemetery I wrote of earlier, though two that do share the name lie buried in the same cemetery some six or seven miles north, not far from the buried remains of the former owner of the Rough Cut. I helped carry both coffins to their holes. One supposes—and I have seen it written as a kind of general truth which may already have passed into the realm of cliché—that one no longer bears one's name both when one is no longer remembered or spoken of or even read about by any living person—and, or so I might add, when the marker indicating that one is buried beneath it, or at least memorialized by it, has been rendered by the elements illegible. When I was recently at the cemetery mentioned so often above I both saw several such graves and even tripped on one. Though I have visited it many times on my own I have only attended one funeral service there (I have been to many at the other). This was five or six years ago. The members of my mother's family had gathered to bury a baby born dead at birth who would have been if she had lived the daughter of my uncle who asked my papa to scatter his ashes along the back side of the ridge on which we were driving when he said this to me, on the day of the first snow in the year after his death. At the service a few words were said in the cold bright sunlight and then the male members of my mother's family including my papa and his brothers buried by hand that coffin shorter than any I have seen before or since. It is 5:35pm as I write these words. My mother was twenty when I was conceived and just married to my father, twenty-eight, who had taken a job at the high school from which my mother had graduated only a little over a year before they'd started dating. Two days after we graduated from college I married my wife at twenty-one. She was twenty-two. We thought it was the right thing. I was around twelve years old when, one day at lunchtime at the school cafeteria, one of my classmates leaned over and helpfully whisper-explained the meaning of a word the other boys were laughing about but which I did not myself understand. That word was *poon*.

Just to the east of the many graves of children of which I earlier wrote—all of whom, it now strikes me, according to a certain doctrine mentioned some pages above, deserved destruction—I saw a fenced-in plot, the wire a deeply rusted red. It was the only fenced-in plot in the entire cemetery. Inside the plot a stone stuck up a mere four or five inches out of the ground, so worn by time and the elements that no name could be read there. Nor hung any identifying marker from the rusted fence or its rusted gate. At the time of the death of the person who now lay there someone had so badly wanted them to be remembered, or at least to make a monument of or to their life, or even to provide them with some semblance of protection, that they'd had a fence constructed. Now only the fence and the unmarked stone indicated the fact that this now-nameless person had ever existed at all. About two months after my wife-to-be and I started dating, during the summer, while we sat on the stoop of the building where he then lived, my father explained to me over a couple of beers how much better sex was if one waited until one was married. Seven or eight years later one of my younger sisters told me she'd found out that our parents had not themselves waited, a fact which my father could easily have confessed but did not confess to me that night on his stoop while we drank. You can't imagine how good it's going to be if you wait, or so he who had not waited said. God, he told me, had designed things this way not only for a reason, His reason, but for our benefit. God has a plan for us, my father said. If we followed that plan, or so my father seemed to be implying, it would lead us to heretofore unknown pleasure. He could have called it the Pleasure of God's Poon for Us. I think I'd likely have been better off if he had.

Last night, two days after having written the initial version of the penultimate paragraph above this one, I spent sixteen or seventeen dollars for the privilege of watching through a screen, in direct response to the money I transferred to her account via a small button, which allowed me to give her a so-called tip, a young woman who placed within her mouth a black rubber ball, which she secured via a small leather harness that went through the ball and tied together at the back of her head. The ball was two or three inches in diameter and rendered speech impossible. Spittle began to leak out of the corner of her mouth, some of the drops of which fell onto the small T-shirt which was the only article of clothing on her body. Earlier today, at dusk, after having lain naked in bed for more than five hours, during most of which time was spent reading *The Magic Mountain,* I put on sweatpants and coat and did a chore Elle had asked me to do. The chore was taking the trash to the dumpster, which is across the street from my building, at the opposite end of the building from our rooms. After tossing the bags into the bin I lit a cigarette and crossed the street, then walked slowly along the sidewalk between my building and the one across the way. Instead of turning right at the door of the apartment I share with my son and Elle, I continued on and up the slight rise into the narrow parking lot to the northwest of my building where I found myself looking up at the three pines which I have earlier so many times mentioned. To my surprise I now found only two pines standing there. The tree nearest my building was as it should be, but there was no tree on the other side of the one which for the five months I've lived here I have taken to be the middle one. Instead, this formerly middle tree, and therefore the Christ-tree of the three, if one considered them, as I have written, to be evocative of that famous scene of crucifixion, fifteen or twenty feet from the ground, bore a branch, as thick as the trunk, which pronged sharply to the west to form a crook that is best described as similar to that of a slingshot. This formerly middle tree, which when seen from my patio had seemed to be two trees, I now realized was actually one tree with two distinct trunks. Three smaller branches jutted straight out of the crook. These three all pointed northeast. The nameless girl whom I last night paid sixteen or seventeen dollars to temporarily render herself unable to speak while wearing only a T-shirt could not see me through her screen but I could see her through mine. My grandfather could see the remains of the boy. The remains of the boy could not see him.

Earlier this year, in the month before I moved with my wife and son into the apartment where we now live, that is to say in May, I began writing what I hoped would become a novel about a sexually inexperienced young man who, along with a voluble older friend, attempts to construct a resort (specifically a lodge, the details of which would be drawn from my imagined version of the one my father attempted to build but which burned down just before it was finished, in the spot where now stands the house of the rich man, which I have, though only in my mind, destroyed by fire) with money inherited from his dead father. In the novel this resort or lodge was to be explicitly devoted to acts of sex and sexual recreation, a sanctuary of sorts for sluts. I made good headway on the novel: ten thousand words appeared in that first and only month of its writing, the sentences arranging themselves in long paragraphs that moved through the text in a braided pattern that pleased me very much, folded together via a method I cannot now entirely recall, but which may very well have been the precursor to the method in use in this very text (perhaps God had a poon for me after all!). Due to various factors, among them the all-consuming act of moving itself, I was unable successfully to return to this novel-in-progress after we had moved into the apartment where I now sit writing these words at just after half-past one in the morning on the thirtieth day of November in the twenty-first year of the new millennium, 1,987 years after the death of the man known by me for the first twenty-one years of my life as the Son of God, one part of the triune entity who created the world and the universe in which it hangs, suspended and rotating along an endless curve not unlike that of a cue ball struck with sharp English. I recently again attempted to take up the manuscript. In the first few days I found success in changing both the main character and his friend into a single character who happened to be a woman with many of the characteristics of the woman in the previous novel mentioned in these pages who spoke of writing a novel in two languages. This second attempt ended shortly after I had written a different version of a scene already described in the earlier pages of this account, of a writer standing at the precise spot in which they'd planned one day to kill themselves, or rather herself, although in that version, which was to be the new version of the novel abandoned back in the summer, I of course used different combinations of words arranged with altogether other architectural structures of syntax and grammar than in the version presented earlier in these pages, the chief architectural difference being that I made a more liberal use of the comma in the novel. (I have begun to weary of the comma and my persistent deployment of it in attempting to cordon off certain of my thoughts from other thoughts.) The other difference is that I wrote of the aforementioned writer standing in the spot where I long ago planned to one day kill myself instead of describing my actual self standing there in that selfsame terminal spot. I say that I paid her sixteen or seventeen dollars. She would've received only half that amount. The other half would go to the online platform that hosted her video feed.

All throughout the afternoon during which I have been revising the above paragraphs, fat flakes of snow have been falling like pieces of torn paper from the sky. When I stepped out for a cigarette about an hour ago one fell upon the space just within the crook between the thumb and forefinger of my left hand, landing precisely on a scar at the base of my index finger, a crook which it now strikes me very closely resembles that of the previously mentioned Christ-tree, the snowflake melting within the space of less than a second, the drop remaining on the left side of the watershed caused by the ridge of the scar, raised at the age of three, as a result of the use of a foldable handsaw under the supervision of my father while cutting a branch: the branch wobbled and the blade jumped off it and into the meat of my tender hand, revealing for a split-second the gray flesh below the skin before the blood spurted out of it. Over these past three decades the scar has remained, and will continue to do so, I suppose, until the flesh falls away from the bone and there no longer remains any *I* attached to it out of which to scream bloody murder for my father. It strikes me now that this description of snow falling like pieces of torn paper has arisen in my mind out of the half-memorized opening page of a novel I first read many years ago, whose opening sentence describes the slow fluttering of many scraps of paper falling through the sky, and which astonished me when I first read it while sitting in the center seat of the empty center aisle of a plane which had lifted me high into the air from the city on the Front Range of the Rockies where I had boarded it and was bound south and east in the direction of my home state. Before buying the book in the airport bookstore where I found it I had just kissed a girl from the Pacific Northwest on the head, the first such contact of my lips with a female person to whom I was not related. I was seventeen and sure, as I read the novel's monumental opening sentence in the empty-but-for-me middle aisle of that 747, that I had just experienced one of the most beautiful moments of my life, still drunk with the aroma of the girl's hair and the softness of it against my lips as my eye followed the immense syntactical pleasure of the novel's first sentence, which described those scraps of paper fluttering through the air as the result of one of the World Trade Center towers being struck by an airplane. I had met the northwestern girl at a two-week-long Christian apologetics camp for teenagers, which was located in an old hotel on the slope of a mountain not far from Pike's Peak. The northwestern girl and I sat those entire two weeks at two adjoining desks—or, rather, not adjoining, for hers was a left-handed desk while mine was right-handed and so they touched. We wrote notes back and forth to each other during almost every hour of each of those fourteen days as various theologians attempted to inoculate us with their variously labored and often byzantine defenses of the faith, which tended to express themselves in the final analysis as some form of gotcha of the incorrigible non-believer. She was the most beautiful girl I had ever seen and the kiss on her head one of goodbye. I dreamed about this girl the night before last, in the sleep that followed my having paid the nameless young woman who was naked from the waist down for the privilege of watching her gag herself with a rubber ball on the other side of my computer screen. In the dream the northwestern girl was naked from the waist up. She spoke to me but I could not understand her, as if the world, or I within it, had gone mute. It was good to see her again. Toward the end of the dream, which no longer seemed to take place via the intermediary space of a screen, as I should say it at first did, but rather in-person, she sat down at a piano set against a wall in deep late afternoon light, the room filled with shadows, where she played a beautiful and melancholic tune which I could neither then nor now identify. Within the dream, which I had by then recognized as a dream, with the absolute certainty that only ever obtains in such oneiric circumstances, I somehow perceived she was playing this music for the express purpose of reminding me of the beauty she had brought into my life. When I woke, relieved of certainty, I was unsure why she'd felt compelled to do this. I no longer think of her often—perhaps a few times a year. I doubt she thinks of me at all. For most of my adult life I've believed that the entities that inhabit our dreams are only ourselves, just as I have increasingly for some time now believed that all of the characters and even the circumstances and landscapes and descriptions there-of in a fiction are always only the author—perhaps especially when they obviously *aren't*. Part of what interests me here about my dream of the northwestern girl I have now not seen in more than a decade, is the sexual desire that I felt for her who was not her in the dream, but also was her, that northwestern girl herself, who was also part of my mind, which is but one part, as I wrote earlier, of the entity I generally consider to be myself. My desire for the character of the northwestern girl in the dream does not now seem to me a desire for myself but rather for another person, who exists nowhere now but in my imagination. But that is not quite right. The northwestern girl exists now as an entity in these pages, and as such has become, like the aforementioned novelist-character, a fiction. As she played the piano, which I now realize stood in a dream version of the house where my parents now live, which stands a little over a mile from where I now write these words at the wrought-iron table, my desire took on a melancholy, even dispassionate mood. What I wanted in the dream, or so I now think, writing this, was the experience of feeling what I had felt sitting at the desk pressed against her desk. But that is not quite right either. What I wanted was to feel again the sweet certainty that that seventeen-year-old version of me had felt on the flight home, reading that expansive opening sentence which so beautifully described one of the great disasters of our time, which itself set the heartbreak of our separation, that of the northwestern girl and myself, that is, in gorgeously tragicomic relief. (What creature more monstrous than a seventeen-year-old in love? While he reads of falling bodies he dreams of romance, and this failure, both his and that of the author who makes it possible, can be said to ennoble further writing. And yet: anything ennobling forms the foundation for future monstrousness.)

While writing the initial version of the above paragraph the day has darkened into night. Snow is falling now through the orange-pink street light that illuminates the small parking lot next to those two pines that seemed until yesterday to be three. That fall the girl sent me letters. First they came regularly and then not at all. I got from this diminishment of correspondence the sense that she must have been living a real life, whereas I sensed that for my part, I lived—if that indeed was the word for it—inside something else. Not real life. Instead: a waiting room at the other end of an adjoining hallway leading nowhere. I felt no bitterness in this realization. Only longing. The dream in which she spoke to me was the first contact she'd made with me in years. Years later I would drive through her hometown on my way to a hiking trip in the Olympic Mountains, and think of her and of those letters I'd sent making their way there, propelled by all the limp force my loneliness could muster.

The letters now lay in a box in one of the closets upstairs, either my son's or the one shared by Elle and I. Of all the things she said to me in the flesh only a handful of statements remain, one of which is a story she told me about her father, after her mother had at that point been dead for a period of several years. She told me that one afternoon her father saw her dead mother standing in their garden. She'd smiled at him, said the northwestern girl. Another time her father saw her dead mother sitting in a chair in the house that the three of them had shared together. When I asked if these visitations were frightening she said that on the contrary, her father found each one comforting. The possibility now strikes me that the characters in both fictions and dreams are in fact living ghosts whose origin is their author, and that when a writer finds manifested in his or her mind or, better, on the page, the presence of a particular character, that this in fact forms a kind of ghostlike visitation of the written self to the writing self. I wonder, two days after having written the initial version of the above sentences of this paragraph, if this spectral awareness may in fact be not unrelated to the act of visiting the grave of some known or unknown person, with name or without, and if, furthermore, the act of writing is in some way similar to kneeling down and trying to brush away the gray-green lichen that has grown over the name on a headstone that has sunk into the soil, as I did when I walked in the cemetery where I hoped, or so I have repeatedly written, one day to have a stone of my own. The lichen was so firmly affixed to the stone that I found it impossible to remove with only my fingers. After looking around for a moment my hand alighted on a small piece of sandstone. I knelt down again and began scraping once more at the lichen, beneath which I saw a cross encompassed by a circle and, below this, the word KOREA. Above the cross and the aforementioned word a name became visible. It was unknown to me, a rarity in this cemetery. I worried as I scratched with the stone in my hand along the surface of the dead soldier's stone that I would deface his name, before I realized it was absurd to imagine that the small piece of sandstone in my hand could deface the surface of the granite rectangle that lay before me, much less the name chiseled there or the date of the soldier's birth, 16 February 1933, two years before my paternal grandfather who in his madness with my father built the now-broken fence along the pines, hoping to turn himself into exactly what he hated, a cowboy. The day of the soldier's death was 30 April 1970. His last day of existence: whatever he had been before then, after that day, a Thursday, he wasn't. My hands are growing cold as I write these words; the three pine trees that are actually two pine trees now form a triune darkness against the darkening sky; twice I myself have seen with my eyes visions of persons who could not have physically been where I saw them in the usual sense. In both visions I saw two people I then longed to see, only later to learn that they could not have been there in the space in which I saw them without some violation having occurred of the laws of space and time. As I worked to remove the lichen that grew upon the soldier's headstone I thought about the curious relationship between defacement and restoration, and wondered what those two boys would have thought if they were to reappear beyond the northern cemetery fence and see me on my knees there, defacing one surface in order to restore the harder surface that lay beneath it, so quietly proclaiming the reality of one man's life. Thirty-seven years.

After completing the initial version of the above paragraph, I wondered, at its conclusion, whether or not the appearance of a ghost might form a defacement of the real. I concluded that the answer was yes. In revising the paragraph I have come to the opposite conclusion. The reason we fear ghosts is that they represent a confirmation, or even better a restoration, of the real—which we cannot bear. Five years. Five years. That's how long lived the boy above whose grave was erected the bench with the words WE LOVED HIM A LOT BUT GOD LOVED HIM A LOT MORE. Writing these words now, repeating for the second time that sentence wrought in iron in an effort at consolation, I can't help thinking that the God that loved him so much was the same God who killed him at the age of five. How could such a concept of love be palatable to anyone? It could only spring from a religion that wholeheartedly endorses the idea of a divine father who sends his own son to the worst kind of slaughter, to be abandoned by his only friends and flayed alive and nailed to a piece of wood and left there until he can no longer draw breath. Christianity frames this story as an act of love for the whole of humanity. For my part I would rather see the whole world rendered a *void* than make such a choice. It seems to me no small wonder, then, that such a religion would both instruct children on the innate evil of their nature and, throughout its history and up to the present day, be the source of wholesale carnage—after all, Christianity's motion, its entire lifeforce, radiates from an act of child sacrifice so terrible that even the so-called heavenly father himself found the scene unbearable, and turned his face from his son, causing him, his boy, nailed there to the heavy tree, the one in the middle, to cry out: *Dad! Why have you forsaken me?* And this Dad, looking down on His son: what did He say? Nothing.

In an earlier paragraph I wrote that I'd carried two coffins to their holes in that cemetery to the north, in which were borne the bodies of two persons bearing the same last name as me. In a fit of propriety I almost changed the word *hole* to *grave*, but in the end decided to leave it as I'd written it: a grave is but a nice word for a hole. The difference in meaning between the words *casket* and *coffin*, by the same token, could be said to be the difference in meaning, with regard to the question of Munch's *Madonna*, of whether it should be described as a great work of art or a great work of smut. One must be nailed shut whereas the other has a hinge. One must be bought. The other may be made at home. Most of the snow has melted now, though until this morning there remained pockets in shadowed places. Even since I was a young boy I have perceived a grim portent in all scenes of melting snow, some awful secret in relation to time itself, and therefore holding some meaning relating to the terms of my own existence, which I had been taught to believe was eternal. The day of the first snow was the one my uncle wanted for his ashes: not, for obvious reasons, the day after. Nothing so much as melting snow implies our own inevitable decay. Its rawness, its epidermis opening as if by gunshot wounds only to reveal the dead grass and mud beneath—that's *us*. That's *our* future. *Your* future. *My* future: *no future*. I wonder if he'd still feel that way now, my papa said. We saw no deer and therefore shot none.

The first time I experienced a visitation, much like the second, I did not know it to be any such thing, for those who visited me were alive, but were not physically-speaking where they were when I saw them (that I saw them with my own eyes ((physically-speaking!)) is the rub). I stood on a stage in a bar with a friend of mine playing a show, the only show we would ever play, to a small crowd comprised entirely of friends of ours, including the young woman I would marry just over two years later. I saw two girls standing at the edge of the crowd, on one of whom I had a crush. I'd written one of the songs explicitly for her, and had imagined playing it while looking into her eyes from the stage, so that when I saw her there at the edge of the crowd I could barely believe how happy it made me feel. And yet, when my friend and I finished our set and came down off the stage, she wasn't there anymore, she wasn't anywhere, and when I asked around where she'd gone, people were confused. Nobody had seen her. Not one person there seemed to know what I was talking about. So I texted her and asked her where she'd gone and she responded by saying she was on the train, headed back from spring break, closing her message with several exclamation marks: Hope we get to see you play!! Everyone there would've recognized her. And I, from the stage, *had* recognized her. Either she and her friend had been standing there or nobody had been standing there, or else I, having seen her standing where nobody was standing, was losing my mind. Later, on the way home from the show, I saw her and her friend walking on the street beside my dormitory, and I texted her again: You back now? Her reply: Nope. Just pulled into the train station. Again, the three other people in the car would've seen her walking there in the street by the dorm. But nobody else saw her and her friend because she and her friend weren't there. I didn't say anything about this to anyone for years. Indeed, I didn't think about it much until it happened again that I saw people where they were not, a few days after the birth of my son, this time in broad daylight. Neither event gave me anything close to the comfort mentioned by the northwestern girl's father. Though we saw no deer and shot no deer we did see a herd of wild pigs. They scattered and ran before my papa could get off a shot because, or so I thought then, sitting beside him in one of his several white pickup trucks, they knew what was good for them. I knew what was good for me, or so I thought then, and so I said nothing about who I'd seen so clearly from the stage.

Since writing yesterday the version of the second-to-last paragraph before this one, I have wondered what cemeteries would be like if there were no names on the stones at all, if cemeteries were to remain exactly as they are, omitting all usage of language and numbers, so that only those who have personally attended the funeral services of the dead or who know those who have done so would know the names of those who lay buried there in near-perfect anonymity, *sine nomine*. It would follow then that if all gravestones were numberless and nameless, nothing would be more natural than for gray-green lichen to expand across their surfaces until the lichen covered each stone completely, nor for the rain and wind and snow and sun of the years to wear down each and every gravestone into nothing larger than a small rock capable of being used to scrape lichen off the surface of a larger one, which act would no longer be necessary nor have any meaning, since if there were no longer any names or numbers on the gravestones there would be no meaning to preserve on the surfaces themselves and indeed nothing for the elements to obscure other than the grave itself, which eventually would be relevant only to gravediggers and cemetery keepers.

Yesterday morning I told my students, to whom I have been speaking for the past few months through the apparatus of a screen, and who still live in the city that my wife and I abandoned earlier this year when we found it impossible to live together there anymore, during our last class session of the semester, after we had finished our discussion of *The Magic Mountain*, that they would remember reading the novel for the rest of their lives. Even if they remembered nothing about the book itself, I said, their memory of the act of reading it would remain. One day, I said, your memory of reading the novel will coalesce into a single memory of a single moment you spent reading it, as my own memory of reading *Crime and Punishment* when I was twenty-one is now of a single afternoon during which I sat for hours on the back patio of a favorite coffee house in the same city in the Pacific Northwest in which the events of the paragraph immediately above this one were described. You will not remember me, I said, when you call to mind this memory. Nor will you remember the contents, or much of the contents, of *The Magic Mountain*. What you will remember is yourself with *The Magic Mountain* lying open in your lap in a particular place and in a particular time. I did not say: this moment will eventually come to perform the same form and function to you as a ghost. It will remain within you and grow stranger and stranger to you, until the person sitting there inside it with the book in their lap has lost everything. (What, you will then wonder, or so I now think, writing this—what happened to you? Did you go into that room? Did you look?) All that will remain of that person, inside the memory, aside from their existence both in and as the image itself, will be the knowledge that the person sitting there with the book had no answers then and has no answers for you now. It's better this way. Leave them alone. They're reading.

Answers or no answers: years from now, or so I thought as I spoke to my students, when they each saw themselves with the book in their lap, ultimately what they would be doing would be calling themselves back to themselves. What the self remembers is always the self, which also happens to be a container for other selves. And yet, my poet friend who suggested I revise the novel I mentioned earlier once told me he was not sure that he had a self at all, in the sense that he was not sure where his own self stood in relation to other selves he had absorbed. I do not know what part of my I is *I*, he might have said, if he were a fictional character instead of my friend the poet, who was born in England and lived out his first decade there, spent most of his second in a cloistered Jewish community near the capital of this country, and lived a few more years of his youth in Jerusalem, although it strikes me that this phrase, not knowing which I is *I*, seems to be torn from the pages of some half-remembered piece of writing not done by me that I cannot now call to mind, rather than something my friend actually said. The things I have written and things others have written often bear the same relation to each other in my head. Often, without at first knowing I am doing so, I type out sentences and parts of sentences that belong, in a sense, in the works of others, although these sentences and parts of sentences seem to belong in an absolute sense in my work as well. It is even possible that this phrase actually originated in one of the many poems written by my friend. If I were to engage him in conversation on this very subject, as I have often done in the past, he might say that the words that I have lifted from his pages he has likewise lifted from others. Earlier this afternoon instead of starting to write when I had originally meant to do so I sent Elle, who was working in the room above me, a text message asking if she wanted me to come upstairs and eat her out. Her response: I want that. Up the stairs I went, and there performed a service for her which might be described as having called herself to herself. Of course, I gained something as well.

As I write these words it is exactly two weeks since I began this account. Sunday. The calendar has changed from November to December. I am typing these words at the wrought-iron table. It is 5:21pm, full dark, though the three pine trees which are two pine trees are visible as a pitch-black form set against the larger darkness of the sky. Yesterday my father sat with me at this table and I mentioned to him the trees, telling him of how I had mistakenly thought of them being not two but three, and that I had been thinking, lately, of the way they evoked for me the three crucifixes as well as the Holy Trinity. He asked me why on earth I had been thinking about this, and I said merely that it had crossed my mind. I said that when I realized they were not three but two I wondered what effect this would have on my mental image of the trees as both the Trinity and the three crosses, and he said that if I bore in mind that the center tree and the one to its right are joined, I could now think of the enjoined trees as being Christ and the thief he promised he would see in paradise that very day. In the Southern protestant tradition in which I was raised, in order to achieve eternal salvation, which is to say to go to heaven after one's death, as the abovementioned thief supposedly did, one must pray a particular prayer inviting Jesus into one's heart. If you pray the prayer—you have to *mean* it—asking Jesus for his forgiveness for your sins, and especially requesting for him to be your Lord and Savior, then Jesus will come to live in your heart. Thus is the decision of one's eternal resting place made. Eternal salvation in heaven is now yours. If you fail to pray this prayer you will go to Hell, or so I was told over and over again, and Hell, or so I was repeatedly told, under no uncertain terms, lasts forever. That this process of committing a literal action might provoke both a spiritual reality and an eventual physical actuality (Heaven or Hell) mimics the processes of magic as conducted in fairytales and old Disney films went entirely unspoken, but I could not escape the intuition that since it was, in fact, a process, one might not be entirely successful on the first try. At a so-called revival when I was seven, I prayed the prayer for the first time. A short while later I was baptized. While at first I felt a great relief in the wake of my decision to ask Jesus into my heart, since it meant that I, too, like the thief, no matter how rotten or sinful I might be, would be granted a heavenly admission, my doubt about the efficacy of my first effort began to grow almost immediately and, scarcely able to dismiss the possibility that, upon my departure from this world and arrival at the gates of heaven, Jesus would shake his head and avert his eyes and send me to the eternal down-below where, as I'd heard it described, the chief activities seemed to be the gnashing of teeth amidst an unending and everlasting darkness, I began to pray the prayer at almost every available opportunity, which was nearly every Sunday. Once, around age twelve if I recall correctly, during the invocation to pray the prayer, I began to feel guilty about an altogether different sort of practice I had recently taken up: taking off all my clothes in bed and lying there in the dark, my hairless dick as hard as a rock, my whole body coursing with a terrified pleasure, until I'd finally had enough, pulled my underwear back on, and fell into a guilty and shame-filled sleep. During this period my days were haunted by the specter of my sin—this *must* be sin, I thought, for why else would my stomach feel like I was carrying a steel ball inside it? During this particular altar call, which took place on an otherwise unnoteworthy Sunday morning, I felt moved in my spirit—such were the only words I then knew to describe what I would now more simply call shame—to confess this act as the sin which I felt certain it was, and I began to cry so profusely that after the service my mother pulled me into one of the empty Sunday School classrooms down the hall from the so-called sanctuary. She seemed concerned, also confused; finally, still crying, I told her what had caused my outburst, and as I now recall this moment I remember that a smile of recognition appeared on her lips, which might accurately be described as similar in appearance to the smile I felt appear on my own after I heard those gunshots at the cemetery almost two weeks ago now. In revising this paragraph, it now strikes me that this smile was one I had also seen on the face of her father.

In appearance I far more resemble those members of my mother's family than my father's. My face is wide rather than narrow like my father's and his father, of whom I have occasionally dreamed ever since his death. My chin, like my papa's, lacks any feature which could be described as prominence. My body is sturdy but fleshy. The only angularity I can be said to possess obtains only when my prick is erect, as it was when I lay naked in bed during those nights of pleasure and fear. At around that age I still hoped one day to be as tall as my mother's brother, who at six-four towered over the rest of the family. One of the earliest memories I have of him is of one bright fall or winter afternoon five or six years before the nights described above. He and his father were sighting in their hunting rifles in my papa's driveway, beyond which lay a pasture full of dead sand-colored grass that was itself bordered by a thick stand of hardwoods. They took their shots; I stood beside my papa. At that moment my uncle was almost certainly younger than I am now as I write these words, two weeks after my papa described to me the manner in which his son had told him of how he wanted his ashes scattered on the first day of the first snow after his death. Their target was a gallon water jug set on a crate in the middle of the road some thirty or forty yards down the driveway. At a certain point, when my papa went inside to fetch something, my uncle took aim and shot the jug off of the crate. He asked me if I would set the jug back up. As I walked toward the crate I felt a tingle of what I did not then know to call anxiety, and I turned around to him my uncle and said please don't shoot. He laughed his boisterous laugh and said: I ain't gonna shoot you! and even though he'd laughed I sensed I'd hurt his feelings in some way, as if in my upwelling of childlike distrust I'd re-opened some old wound, as if I'd somehow denied him his status as my uncle, and therefore as his sister's brother, and still further as his father my papa's son—and yet, it occurs to me now, writing this, that I may have invented this laughter of my uncle in order to assuage my own guilt for having possibly caused him to feel dislocated from and within his own life. It's far more likely that I blew the entire experience out of proportion and my papa's son felt none of what I have described above. And yet: the noting of my guilt as a possible invention may itself also be an assuagement—but what part of all that one writes is not, ultimately, an assuagement? All writing satisfies one or another desire in the writer. Recently while alone in the shower I violated myself with a kitchen implement. It is possible that this act, of which I will for now spare the reader further detail, also constituted an assuagement of sorts. My papa told me not to look but I wanted to look and, if only for a moment, did so. I ain't gonna shoot you.

For many years I suspected that it was the quality of one's *no* by which the final assessment of one's character must be made—that it was one's apophatic relation to life that matters. It may be this exact perspective, which I have long imagined was inherently skeptical in nature, which has for much of my life prevented me from fully embracing certain aspects of my character and habits of my person that past versions of myself described in this account could not have failed to find unsavory or even immoral. After ejaculating in the shower I washed the kitchen implement with soap and hot water. Recently while using the internet I learned that there was such a thing as a so-called anal hook, but did not learn precisely what it was or what function such an object might play in the production or action of increasing one's pleasure. What did I avert in failing to learn this? The person with *Crime and Punishment* lying open in his lap had no answers then and has no answers now.

Up until about six months ago I had never seen a ball gag. The first time I saw one also happened to be the first time I logged onto the website that I use from time to time in order to pay young women to commit acts of a sexual nature for my own benefit and, one supposes, the benefit of others watching. (Why did I instinctually use the word *benefit* and not *pleasure*? This feels to me now, writing these words, like a glimpse into another old habit of mind. The word *benefit,* despite or perhaps because of its financial sense, carries with it the implication of moral goodness, and thus of its own justification. It is a word which could be said to stand upright, whereas the word *pleasure* carries within it both the sound and outward appearance of the word leisure and thus implies lying down, idleness, immorality.) I have just briefly, before the initial writing of the past two sentences, logged onto the website again, where I saw with pleasant recognition the same large-breasted woman who was the first person I ever saw place such an object into the largest orifice of her face and bind it with a leather buckle behind her head. The room in which she appeared both then and just now seemed to be a bedroom with wooden floors and paneling, the ceiling inclining slightly on both the right and the left, as if it were the top room in a wooden cabin not so different from the one in which I spent most of my childhood and in which I just over two weeks ago began writing this account. On both viewings the room looked like a comfortable place to spend a quiet afternoon naked in bed with a book, similar to the afternoon during which just over a week ago I spent the whole day naked in bed, reading that overlong novel about the goings-on of a particular sanatorium which, in my imagination, appeared far different from the former sanatorium and now former hospital in which I was myself born. I am not sure to what use the building is put now, if any. The implement to which I referred above no longer finds itself stored in the kitchen and as such may need a new name. Does a spoon remain a spoon always?

Just now the contrail of an airplane flying at an almost unimaginably high elevation has crossed against the highest point of the Christ-trees which are now pressing black against the lavender sky directly to the west of where I sit writing these words. The contrail, which has thinned a bit since I finished writing the initial version of the previous sentence, possesses the color of coral and is, or rather was, when the sight of it compelled me to begin writing the previous sentence, quite beautiful. When I logged onto the website mentioned in the previous paragraph the aforementioned woman whom I once saw gag herself was wearing a pretty gray dress and chatting amicably into the camera. I did not have my sound turned on and therefore did not hear the words she was speaking. I wonder now if, when I dreamed of the northwestern girl speaking to me through the screen while naked from the waist up, had I the ability to press some or another key, I would have understood what she said. I rarely encounter such screens or keys in my dreams, for in my dreamlife it is generally the case that all technology invented after my immediate childhood either does not exist or at least seems not to, much as is the case in most of the works of fiction I read, which generally were published in the years before I came into existence or else have been written by living writers who studiously avoid making mention of such technology out of fear, one supposes, that they might be identified as living authors. The aforementioned dream, in which the northwestern girl at first appeared to be on the other side of a screen, may have been for me the first of its kind. I now recall that when I watched the young woman naked from the waist down, and made mention for the first time in this account of that item used to render her person incapable of coherent speech, I did in fact have the sound turned on, and I heard that young woman call the item before she placed it in her mouth and bound it with the buckle at the back of her head not a ball gag, but a *gag ball*.

A few days before embarking on the trip westward to the state in which I was born and the house in which I spent most of my growing-up years, in which I would much later begin writing this account, the lens that I use to see clearly out of my right eye popped out of the frame of my glasses. In the moment before it fell completely out of the frame it turned slightly in the frame and I experienced an aberration of vision caused by the angle of the lens in relation to my right eye. Through the use of duct tape I managed to sustain the position of the lens inside the frame for the duration of the trip that began a little over a day later, as well as for most of the ten or so days that followed. Exactly one week ago, after returning to the city in which we now live, after picking up my son from the daycare he attends two days a week, I took my duct-taped glasses and myself and my son to an optometrist's office and asked could my glasses be repaired. A sharply-dressed older man endowed with the soft Southern accent common to this region inspected my glasses. His inspection took but a moment. He reported that the news was grave. However, he said, he could check and see if my lenses would fit any of the extra frames he had lying around, which I presumed to be the kind that had either been donated or marked not for sale. When I expressed that I found the idea agreeable he reached under a desk and pulled out a large cardboard box filled with frames, most of them already containing lenses, piled higgledy-piggledy all the way to the top. He set the box on the floor and dug in it much the same way as a child will dig in a toybox for a particular car or dinosaur. After a moment or two he made an indistinct noise indicating his failure to find that for which he searched, the same sort of sound which, though common enough in basic interactions, is also one of the only communicative noises which can be made by one who has either placed or had placed into one's mouth a gag, either including or not including a rubber ball. The man replaced the box beneath the desk and then disappeared through a doorway. A few minutes later he returned with the frames I now wear and through which I am looking as I write these words. He popped the lenses from my formerly duct-taped glasses into this new set, which did not appear new at all, but were an old-fashioned pair of gold wireframes. These will get you by for now, he said.

Though grateful for these frames because they allow me to see the various objects and personas with which my gaze comes into contact when illuminated by some or another light source, I have found, toward the end of each day since the optometrist gave them to me, an increasing desire to take them off and set them aside, for the ends of the arms—if that is the correct term—dig into the skin just behind each of my ears, and this continual impingement invariably results in a headache. Earlier today, before I began to write the initial version of this paragraph during the noon hour, sitting at the wrought-iron table, instead of writing I opened a short work of prose fiction that I have been reading for most of the two weeks and more since I began the composition of this account, in the house in the state where I was born, on the day I went hunting with my papa for the first time in over a decade. I had not read more than a few pages before it occurred to me that I could postpone the onset of the pain behind and between my ears as I was reading through the simple act of setting for a short time my new though rather old-fashioned glasses on the wrought-iron table. Without glasses I can see with ease that which is only twelve-to-eighteen inches from my eyes, although anything either nearer or farther away tends to blur. As I sat reading, able to view the letters of each word of each sentence of each paragraph of the book with the utmost clarity, when I looked up from the book at the now-blurry Christ-tree and its one or two neighbors to the west of my patio, I experienced a sensation I'd once found utterly indispensable but which I had not made the habit of seeking out in more than a decade. I call this sensation *the blur*.

In the year or two before I first began to wear glasses I often experienced when hunting with my father or my papa a deficiency of vision that I did not know to be so. When my father or my papa pointed out some animal in the woods, say a turkey or a deer, I found to my increasing dismay that I could only rarely spot it, and even then I could apprehend the creature in question only by virtue of some sudden movement. By the time I reached the age of fourteen my parents or my grandparents or both had apprehended the fact that I was in need of glasses and I was given my first set of wireframes, which I chose from a wall of frames in the optometrist's office of the hospital that replaced the sanitorium or asylum in which I was born. I well recall putting on the glasses in the passenger seat of our family car. What awe I felt in the clarity of the pine trees that stood beyond the parking lot! That it was now possible to make out the details of each bough and even the individual needles oscillating in the mild breeze filled me with pleasure. And yet, soon after entering the bristling world of sight, I discovered a converse pleasure: that of removing the glasses to allow my vision to return to the state of blur which had previously defined, or rather failed to define, every object or person or thing at which I directed my gaze. My vision again entered this state when I removed my glasses this morning and looked up at the now-blurry Christ-tree and its one or two neighbors to the west of my patio. This experience, upon discovery, produced in me a feeling of heightened concentration not unlike that which I would later experience in the immediate moment after first drawing on a lit cigar or cigarette. Throughout the remaining years of my adolescence I often found solace in taking off my glasses and looking at or rather *into* the blurred world I then found before my eyes, for this caused me to experience the sensation that there no longer existed any division between myself and the world at which I looked. Clarity of vision produces definition and definition produces meaning. This is not always desirable. To be relieved of the need to define is to be relieved of the endless sorting process of meaning-making; and yet, or so it strikes me now, this kind of relief, no longer much remarked upon or especially valued in our time, was once called *repose*. Certain Christian denominations still sing hymns about resting in the Lord: to rest in the Lord is to be at one with him. It now seems to me that to look with blurred vision into the world is no longer to be separated from the world but rather immersed both in it and *of* it, remaking the world into a kind of womb. But here the idea breaks down. To be within the womb is to be protected from the world and carries the implication not so much of immersion but of infancy. And yet this is precisely what Christ commanded of his followers: be ye as children, he said, and they were, and they are.

When I thought of this act of glasses-removal while looking up from reading the work of prose fiction mentioned earlier, I immediately recalled to myself the image of myself in the center seat of the center aisle of that airplane carrying me homeward from the mountainous state wherein I had moments before, for both the first and last time, kissed on the head the northwestern girl who would much later appear to me in a dream, as I sat there reading the long opening sentence of that novel which described the torn bits of paper falling through the sky—an act of reading from which I reposed by removing my glasses and staring up at the gray blur of the ceiling of the plane, my thoughts full of the northwestern girl—though this I would first recall only on the first day of this year's first snow, as suddenly overwhelmed with emotion as I had been when I permitted the novel I was reading to fall closed into my lap and removed my glasses while I flew in the opposite direction from the northwestern city where I would one day stand on a stage and glimpse two young women who were not in fact standing where I saw them standing only a few feet away from the woman who would become my wife, who would gently laugh at me upon my confession of the discovery, made more than a decade later, that my member could be made to stand to attention at the sight of another man's doing so.

I do not know where or when I got out of my habit of looking into the blur. It is likely that, as with most habitual actions performed in order to produce the feeling or at least the illusion of meaningfulness, I experienced a gradual diminishment in its efficacy or intensity. It's possible that I simply became so accustomed to viewing the world through my glasses that any value produced by intentionally inhibiting my own clarity of vision became lost to me. After all, once I'd received my first pair of glasses, to take them off was, in a sense, to travel backward in time to the period when all I was capable of seeing when I looked farther afield than the distance of a book held in front of my face comprised a collage of indistinct particulars. The simplest explanation is most likely: that I began to seek out the same feeling formerly incurred via the experience of blurred vision via other means, such as through the habitual actions mentioned both obliquely and directly some pages ago in which I described certain aspects of my character and habits of my person that past versions of myself described in this account could not have failed to find unsavory or even immoral, such as those involving certain monetary-sexual interactions or kitchen implements, given that those past versions of myself were devoted to the pursuit of a relationship with the entity that the boy and later the young man regarded as both the creator of the universe and that creator's son, both of whom the man, once he was no longer so young and no longer believed the entity to be anything more than a fiction or fictions, would later find evoked by the two pine trees that he had by then for many months thought of as three, at which he'd often had occasion to glance up from his work and gaze at through the lenses of his glasses, glasses the frames of which would break shortly before he began to write the initial versions of many of the sentences found in the pages above.

Earlier in this account I wrote that for most of my adult life I've believed that the entities that inhabit our dreams are only ourselves. I added thereafter that I have increasingly for some now time believed that all of the characters in a work of fiction are always only ever the author, perhaps especially when they obviously aren't, and I further speculated that the characters in both fictions and in dreams are in fact living ghosts whose origin is their author, the writer or the dreamer, so that when a writer finds a particular entity manifested in his or her mind or on his or her pages—or now, I think, writing these words, in his or her dreams—this manifestation forms, in fact, a kind of ghostly visitation. I further speculated that this spectral awareness might be in some way related to the act of visiting the grave of some person known or unknown, named or possibly nameless, though I did not then remark upon the apparent incongruity of the phrase *living ghosts*.

The second time I saw people who were not in fact where they were when I saw them—and who were therefore, despite their vivid appearance, not actual living people at all—was, as mentioned earlier, shortly after the birth of my son. This event took place around noon on a bright and cloudless day in the northwestern city where I was then living with the mother of my child, only a couple of miles from that hill which I earlier mentioned frantically running down in an attempt to escape certain imagined acts of a sexual nature with a young and amply-bosomed woman. The sun shone clear and bright, midday in midsummer, and I was standing alone in the living room of our apartment looking down onto the sidewalk that ran between our building and the next when I saw my mother and father coming down the walkway in the direction of our front door. My son had only been in the world about three or four days, and I was glad to see them, my parents, for I greatly desired to see what I'd always previously regarded as the natural order of things restored, however briefly, which is to say I wanted to regain the sense that I myself was not in the position of parent but rather that of child. Because we frequently had trouble with our buzzer, upon seeing my parents I immediately exited the apartment, boarded the elevator and took it the one floor down, where I opened the glass door and walked outside. Neither my father nor my mother were anywhere to be found. I stepped out onto the walkway and looked in both directions. Nothing. The building had entrances on both the south and north ends, and I thought maybe they'd already tried the buzzer and then headed for one of those. I circled the building. They were not at the south end, nor at the north. I texted my mother and asked her where they were, thinking they might've forgotten something in their car and gone back to get it. She responded immediately: they were still at the apartment they'd rented for the week, several miles to the east of where I then stood. All this took less than a couple of minutes. Dumbfounded and alarmed, I lit a cigarette. While I smoked I decided not to mention what had happened to anyone. After all, I'd slept very little or at best only very intermittently over the past few days. I thought of the moment when from the stage I saw the young woman with whom I was enamored and her friend at the edge of the crowd. As there were no less recognizable people in the world to me than my parents, it seemed impossible for me to have mistaken two random strangers for them. From my window to where I'd seen them walking was a distance of less than fifty feet, and as I write this now I realize there was another congruity with the previous time I saw people who were not there: the angle of sight. I saw both pairs of people from above. In either case, though, my eyes could hardly be faulted, for one does not mistake the beloved nor those without whom one would not have come into being to start with. As during the former instance, in wanting to see them there, I therefore saw them there, and in both cases, or so I now think, writing this, what I saw was my desire. In another sense what I saw was *myself*. What relation this bears, if any, to the desire of the heavenly father looking down at the suffering of the son and turning his face away from him who was simultaneously himself, I do not know. In reviewing this paragraph upon its final lines, it strikes me that the use of the word *therefore* three sentences ago merits interrogation.

After completing the initial versions of the most recent couple of paragraphs, which completion was followed by eating a meal of spaghetti and meatballs both with my parents and with my son, my wife and I set up between ourselves in bed the device on which I am now writing these words. We positioned it to where we could both see the screen. I logged into the website I sometimes use to pay women in various states of deshabille to perform acts of a sexual nature, and together we found online a woman about our age whom I had watched and paid a number of times before but whom I have not yet mentioned in these pages. She wore a maroon cardigan over a black leotard and sat cross-legged on what appeared to be her bed while smiling and speaking into the camera as if talking to persons who were also visible on the other side of it. At one point she turned and greeted a person in the actual room with her, or just outside of it, perhaps a roommate just arriving home, passing by the doorway to her room. On the bed in our room Elle wore nothing. I also wore nothing. I asked her what she wanted to do. She said she wanted to see someone doing something sexy. I said we could ask the woman on the screen to do something. To do so we only had to acquire some of the digital currency used to pay performers, then make a tip with the request for the specific action. Elle said she would like to do just that, so I did: eleven dollars for a hundred tokens. We looked at the woman's tip menu. She's so pretty, Elle said. I thought you would like her, I said. We tipped the amount designated for the woman, who ostensibly was located in a state that borders the ocean far to the west of here, to expose her breasts, and she pulled down her leotard, pressed her tits together and began caressing them with her hands. Oh my God, Elle said. She started touching herself. Oh my God, she said. I started touching myself. I watched Elle touch herself. The woman on the screen was sitting cross-legged on her bed. We were laying on either side of our bed. I could tell Elle was nervous to be taking such obvious pleasure in watching another woman. I said: You should enjoy yourself. Elle seemed to begin enjoying herself. A few minutes later the woman on the screen pulled her leotard back up and reached back to the nightstand at the corner of her bed, where she'd set a mug of tea, which she now sipped and began describing for her audience. I cannot now, writing this, recall the kind of tea—perhaps it was dandelion—but Elle seemed so excited by the fact of the tea, and the woman in the far western state's persistent drinking of the probably dandelion tea, not to mention her ongoing description of it, that it seemed to produce an entirely new feeling of ecstasy in Elle. Drink that fucking tea, Elle said. Drink that fucking tea, she said again. I laughed.

Oh my God she is drinking that tea, she said, she's drinking that dandelion fucking tea, she said, and came. A moment later she reached over and took my penis in her hand and started pleasuring me, continuing to narrate the pleasure she was taking in watching the woman on the screen drinking her fucking tea as she continued to chat charmingly with the camera in response to questions or comments made by members of her audience that appeared in text form on the screen before both her and us. I asked her if she wanted to ask the woman on the screen to wear a ball gag. She said yes and started to make the tip request. Wait, I said, we should let her finish her tea first! Elle laughed. She continued to pleasure me. A moment later the woman on the screen set her tea aside in a way that seemed definitive. We made the request accompanied by the tip, and the woman on the screen said she would have to look for it. She went off camera briefly and we heard the sound of something like chains in the background, which sound caused Elle to shiver with pleasure. I asked her if she wanted me to take her from behind while we watched. Yes please, she said. She slid the laptop forward on the bed and got on her hands and knees in front of the screen. The woman on the screen placed the ball in her mouth and started to affix the strap. I slid myself inside Elle, gently massaging her back and shoulders with my hands, and began to gently thrust. The woman on the screen finished affixing the strap. I thrusted more forcibly. Elle moaned. The woman on the screen massaged her tits, which she'd brought back out as the result of someone else's tip. I fucked Elle. Elle fucked me back. We both watched the woman on the screen. I suddenly wished that I hadn't asked Elle if she wanted to ask the woman on the screen to use the ball gag—after all she'd been enjoying listening to her talk, and the woman on the screen, too, had seemed to enjoy talking. Oh well, I thought, thrusting, it's too late now, and in that brief moment of my regret the woman in the western state leaned forward to show a stream of spittle leaking over her lower lip and onto her chin and my feeling of regret altogether vanished; I thrusted harder than before, and came. From the sounds Elle made, so did she, for a second time. The woman on the screen removed the gag, smiled, wiped her mouth in one delicate motion with the back of her hand, and resumed talking to the camera as if nothing out of the ordinary had happened. For a few minutes afterward Elle and I lay on the bed watching her talk. Oh my God, Elle said again. She is so sexy. *That* was so sexy. Do you want to keep watching her, I asked. Maybe, she said, do you? We lay naked on our bed and watched the woman on her own bed in the far western state talk to the camera, her breasts exposed above her black leotard. After a moment or two I finally got up and started to get dressed. Elle reached forward and closed my laptop. Slipping on her bathrobe, she said: Better not leave this on unless he gets up. A moment later she poked her head into the boy's room. She whispered my name. Look at him, she said. I looked: he lay sleeping on his back with his arms extended in either direction, both utterly babylike and also as if he had, in his slumber, reached the height of some kind of drunken ecstasy. He's so beautiful, she said. Afterward, smoking on the patio, she said: I've never let myself get that turned on by a woman. I've never come from watching a woman before. I said I was glad she had. I felt happy, and said so. There was a short pause in our conversation. I wondered if it was true that I felt happy. (This all happened well before the day at the beach where I saw myself rise at the rising of the young man: as such I did yet not know that I, too, possessed the capability for a similar excitement.) Probably,

I said to myself, yes, I think so. We smoked. I asked her what she thought of what we'd just done. She said she was still thinking about it but that she'd definitely enjoyed it. Though I wanted to ask her more, I recalled an observation of Emil Cioran's to the effect that we do not reflect with impunity on that which by its very nature dispenses with reflection, *i.e.* the orgasm, for the interrogation of the erotic by means of the intellect risks the destruction of the very aspect which brings the erotic into being and enables its existence. I did not ask her more.

For many years I muzzled my desire and spent the entirety of my twenties trying to find relief from it through the outlet of the written word. Instead of seeking access to the inner blur of my own sexuality, I tried to make for myself a world of language. (That sexuality falls beyond or rather outside language seems to me the reason that the sex act is so resistant to literary representation, and is what renders it the least inherently literary of all human phenomena, while at the same time lending itself so beautifully to cinema: the moving image describes but does not explain, while the very act of explanation forms the entire basis of the existence of language. This explains why literary representations of sex that are overly successful, so to speak, are often seen as gratuitous or even downright pornographic, whereas pornography, gratuitous by nature, once placed under the burden of explanation, both suffers and ends by yielding its oneiric power. It's for this reason, I think, that I've stuffed this text with dreams.) I spent most of the rest of the decade that followed the night I ran headlong down the hill from the bar trying to convince myself that I did not know what I knew that I knew about myself—this is not even to speak of certain things I did *not* know about myself which would be brought to light by such an interrogation as that which obtains in this text.

One night during grad school, out drinking with other members of my cohort, everyone but me decided to leave the bar and head to the town's only strip club. When asked why I wasn't going, too, I said simply that I didn't want to. The inevitable follow-up question: was it that my wife wouldn't let me go? No, I said. It wasn't that she wouldn't let me. The reason I wouldn't go, besides not being all that interested, or so I said, was that I didn't want to put my wife in the situation of being asked if I could go. Besides, I said again, I didn't want to. It's hardly worth remarking that this thrice-repeated statement was a lie. Or that when I said I didn't want to put my wife in the position of answering the question of whether or not I could go to the strip club, what I was really saying was that I didn't want to put *myself* into the situation of outright lying both to my wife *and* myself at the same time. Lying to myself felt bad enough. Instead, on this night and others, when I watched the other young men my age doing the things that other young men my age typically did, I told myself I was more mature than they were. I was *married*, after all, while nearly all the others in my cohort, being in their early-to-mid-twenties, like I was, were single. Somehow I managed to convince myself that this lack of tail-chasing on my part equated both to my possession of an innately stronger moral character and likewise meant I was more committed to being a writer than any of them—at which point, left drinking alone at the bar while they dashed off to the club, laughing, I went home, found my wife asleep, and furtively whacked off onto a towel. Still later, on an evening the following year, as I chatted in the beer garden of the department bar with one of the most beautiful women I had ever seen, another writer in the program, I felt like God Himself was squatting on my back, waiting for that first impurity of thought, and fought the urge, again, to run. I'm here to write, I said, I'm here to write, I'm here to write, not here to try to fuck every (read: any) girl in the program. I imagined the woman's lips against mine and then against other parts of me and was relieved, finally, when my drink was empty and I had an excuse to break off our conversation. (By this point I'd at least managed to learn that one need not *run from* the bar, particularly if there were others around. One could simply relocate.) My virtue acted as a mask for my vanity, my vanity formed a mask for my fear, and my fear lay as a bedfellow with my torment. In short: my balls hurt. The more they hurt, the more I told myself they did not hurt. I may as well have cut them off. My papa told me not to look and I can truthfully say that for many years I followed orders.

A few pages earlier in this writing I mentioned that a certain usage of the word *therefore* merited interrogation. Apropos Cioran's warning that we do not reflect with impunity on that which by its very nature dispenses with reflection, I think that one does not think about sex if one thinks about sex, but rather something entirely distinct from it, any more than to think about firing a gun is to actually fire one. There is nothing theoretical about pleasure. (In the initial writing of the previous sentence I wanted to add: just as there is nothing theoretical about life.) While both illusory and fleeting in nature, the orgasm an illusion never is. It either happens or it does not happen. Sexual pleasure can and even ought to be described, but it cannot be explained. Even if an explanation were possible, it would have no bearing on the pleasure itself, or be so far removed from it as to be about an altogether different topic—the explanation of pleasure via the actions of endorphins in the brain bears no more relation to the experience of pleasure than would reading the description of the molecular makeup of fried chicken compare to the pleasure of eating it. That which is inexplicable about sex is precisely what makes sex pleasurable. Indeed, its lack of explicability may be said to account for a great deal of the virtually constant moral anxiety about sex throughout recorded history. In the absence of explanations there is no *therefore,* and without *therefore,* no morality. If we cannot assign motives to these feelings or desires then we cannot say whether they are right or wrong. The genitals have no consciousness, and consciousness, no matter how much we might wish the case to be otherwise, has no authority over the genitals: ultimately, what the genitals have in common both with the brain and the heart which beats time between them is that there is very little in the human heart that can be explained but much that can be described. When a solitary man asks his father for his ashes to be spread on this or that slope on the far side of this or that ridge on the first day of the first snow after his death, he does not explain but rather describes himself.

The orgasm produces not perfect silence but rather the moan, grunt, and whimper of the creature, pulling the human beyond his or her own volition into an inner blur that lies just beyond language. Words are not life. They are its adjunct. In most cases, or so I now think, writing this, they are also the mask we slide over life to prevent ourselves being injured by it. Cioran writes in his *Précis de décomposition* that it is the use of concepts which makes us masters of our fears. By concepts he means words, which insulate us from reality. If he can be believed, and I increasingly think he can, then that which lies beneath a word will always defy and even destroy any understanding of what that word represents. In the *décomposition,* the first of his books written not in his native Romanian but in French, a language previously unknown to him, he refers to this space beneath the word as *the unqualified universe*. The word itself, he tells us, is an attempt to escape misery and even death. Through it, like our first father there in the garden, Adam, we baptize the world—which is to say we immure ourselves from it. This for Cioran is the torment of language, or rather the torment language both enacts and attempts to ameliorate, for language functions much as a baptismal font, clothing the pure terror of the absolute (which we might describe as speechless, unspoken, or silent, and be right on all three counts) with a raiment we imagine we may grip with our own hands. In this way language equips us with both a texture that we use to grapple with the slippery nature of the world and an imaginary escape route *from* that world. It is something to hold on to because we *imagine* we hold onto it. Thus: an illusion. What Cioran fails to note is that pleasure, too, lies beyond both thought and language. The unqualified universe makes pleasure possible in the first place. Even if we may wish for our ashes to be spread here or there, or our lives to be ended here or there, we can never truly fathom not existing at all; likewise, it is orgasm's delirious excision of self from self that gives sexual pleasure its awesome power: that for the length of a single moment, or several such moments, we are relieved of the burden of being ourselves—after which we may lie back on the bed with our lover, watching the person on the screen continue to talk or to drink that fucking tea, and in so doing, as we gasp for breath, be returned to ourselves.

I can still remember that particular gasp of sensuality, not the first but near it: the pastor gently placing his hand upon my shoulder as he proclaimed to the congregation, which occupied three columns of pews not unlike the seating of a 747, with my paternal grandfather and grandmother in the third pew of the middle column, and my parents seated at the front of the column to my right, with my maternal grandparents seated some number of rows of pews behind them, that I had been saved. With one hand upon my chest and the other behind the back of my head, he then dipped me into the water, fully immersing my body as required by his version—my parents' version and *a posteriori* mine—of the faith, and brought me back to the surface to applause. I gasped for air and wiped the water from my eyes. Cioran describes Adam as baptizing the world through naming it. My pastor, in baptizing me, publicly set the name of Christ upon my head. When Cioran died I was only five, living with my mother and father in a trailer house owned by the public high school and elementary where my father taught science and coached basketball. A few years ago, while reviewing an English-language reissue of the above-named book for the *Times Literary Supplement*, I came across an account by one of his translators from his first language, who said that when Cioran died he could not speak a single word, not even those words which belonged to no language at all: his own name. He had long planned to avoid senility through suicide, or so wrote his translator, but when he lost the ability to speak, Cioran, who wrote first in one language and then in another, lost what I would call his place by the river, and so lived out his last days gagged by the weight of his long life, unknown even to himself, suspended in a nameless amber, still breathing, as did my paternal grandfather, who with my father once built a barbed wire fence down by the river in an attempt to cordon off his madness from himself, ultimately surviving more than two decades past the grim morning when my father found him lying face-down on a waterbed in the pre-dawn dark with a pistol pressed against his temple and his finger on the trigger. That room, in which I usually slept when staying the night at my grandparents' house, though I then knew nothing of what had happened there, always seemed to have something wrong with it. In the adjoining bathroom was a red heat light above the bathtub. When turned on at night this light radiated a satanic glare that reached ominously into the bedroom and was all too easy for my six-year-old mind to imagine emanated from the mouth of hell. This sentiment was too close to the heart of the matter. Hell really had come to that room. It entered my grandfather's mind there, where my father found him and took the gun from his hand, driving him that very morning to a mental hospital in Tulsa called, of all things, Laureate, a word which in its adjectival form literally means to be wreathed as a mark of honor, where he would be given a pair of plain black slippers without laces. Years later, only a few moments after his death, as he lay dead on the hospital bed, my grandmother asked if my grandfather's mouth could be closed. The gravity of the turning earth refused her request. She held onto his unfeeling hand and wept.

One night about a month ago, a full month after I had last made an entry in these pages, and more than six months ago as I write the initial version of this paragraph in late September of the year after I began this account, I found myself sitting across from him, dead three years now. We were sitting at the dining room table of the house he lived in when I was a boy, in the room directly above the one in which my father found him gun-to-head. At the beginning of the dream were just sitting together, though I cannot recall whether or not we spoke. All of a sudden his hands began to tremble, as they often did in the last years of his life, and then they started shaking even more, as if he were having a seizure, and I jumped out of my chair to try to help him, but I could not help him, just as no one had ever been able to help him, and his body began to swell, and kept swelling, until it was as if his head were a sausage on a grill, at which he point he fell on the floor and burst. The colorless fluid that escaped his broken epidermis—which, to my horror, seemed to be his life force or spirit—felt warm to the touch, cooling rapidly on the linoleum and leaving behind only his shriveled skin, the shriveled skin of my dead grandfather there on the floor of his dining room, wrinkled and empty. It strikes me now that the fluid was much the same temperature and just as soft as the baptismal water into which I'd been plunged as a boy. The body of Christ, the preacher said, gently lowering me into the font which felt like liquid silk, now resurrected to walk in a new life. And all God's people said amen, said the preacher. The congregation said it with him. Amen. After his death I found those black laceless shoes in his closet and was both awestruck and horrified that he'd kept them, and, on a trip to that far northwestern city, horrified myself by wearing them up and down its dizzyingly steep hills in the rain until they were worn completely apart and my feet covered in blisters. Everything sane inside me said not to enter that room. Following my father I walked in anyway and, finding it unbearable, removed those shoes from my feet in that damp city and dropped them in a trash can.

Less than two weeks after its first iteration I had the same dream of him swelling and exploding, and again at its end all that was left of him my grandfather resembled more closely the remains of a busted water balloon than those of a person. This morning I dreamed of an old friend who lay with her naked body pressed against the back of my naked body. I lay on my belly and she lay on my back. I can't guarantee you anything, she said. I whispered back: You know I'd never ask you to. In a later scene in the same dream my wife seemed onto what was going on between my old friend and me. I could tell she was upset from the way she refused to say anything about it. For some reason the dream itself took place at the house in which my mother and her brother were raised, and in which my papa and granny still lived when I was a boy, and still stands about a mile as the crow flies from the fallen-in ruin of the gas station and video rental once known as the Rough Cut. The remains of my grandfather have lain for more than three years in the same cemetery as that of the murdered man, as do those of my papa's father and mother, and many of my other relatives going back more than a century. I do not wish to be buried there myself.

My balls hurt, or so I wrote toward the end of one of the above paragraphs, referring to my time in grad school, and the more they hurt, the more I told myself they did not hurt. In those days sleep brought no relief from this pain, as it had in the years which accompanied my first set of wireframe glasses, through which I looked and saw the bristling world so clearly. At fourteen I lay my new glasses on the shelf beside my bed and prayed without quite addressing God Himself for that relief which was the only one for which I was certain I could not be held accountable: an image and a spasm and that was it. Each wet dream felt like a special dispensation. I'd read the dictionary definition of ejaculation, but I was utterly in the dark as to how it came about. I knew from the scriptures that Onan spilled his seed on the ground and that the Lord found this act to be an abomination. Just *how* Onan spilled it remained a mystery. Intuition told me it in no way resembled knocking over a glass. Around the same time my father sharply informed me that in the eyes of God, masturbation or indeed any form of sexual activity that occurred outside of a context with one's spouse was a form of *adultery*. It was a word which could not fail to occur without italics. *Adultery*. Like Cain with his horn, I imagined being marked by it forever, and shuddered. The orgasm, then: the sacred and exclusive provenance of intercourse within the context of holy matrimony. And yet—I forget how or where I discovered this—one of the next things I learned about sex was that the act could be conducted in the exact same posture as dogs! and cattle! and horses! This mortified and ashamed me on behalf of all humanity. The idea that we could do it *like dogs*—drooling and woofing—and *cows* and *bulls* and *horses*—mooing and bawling and snorting—without even looking at each other—in, say, the middle of a pasture—didn't this run counter to all ideas of the sacred? This was not a thought I allowed myself to think, though I thought it anyway, while simultaneously forbidding myself from doing so. (A taste for the impossible: shared enthusiasm both of writers and certain inmates of mental asylums.) At a church camp at seventeen I listened to a preacher talk for more than an hour about the dangers of sexual sin and then, toward the end of the service, as the altar call music began to play, instruct all the teenagers there assembled to shut their eyes. (Did he imagine coming on all our faces at once, I now wonder.) Make eye contact with me, he said, if you've committed some secret sin. Look up, he said, if you ain't right with God. Lock eyes with me if you're committing some secret sin right now. Look up, he said. I felt that if I didn't look up, God would crush me right then and there into the floor, and opened my eyes and raised my face to see if that would provide any relief from the sensation. It did not. Once, that same year or the one after, after I'd been hired to work as temporary staff for a Christian political camp, a month before the program was to start I received a phone call from one of the permanent staffers—a teenager himself, though he felt lightyears older than me simply by virtue of the authority conferred upon him by being the maker of the call. He had only one question. Had I looked at any pornographic material in the past year? Unless a certain French film called *Swimming Pool* counted, I had not, but my conscience said that I should say yes—it would have said yes no matter what, I think. Trembling all over, I said yes. The line went silent for a moment. I asked if this would disqualify me from participating in the camp. I'm not sure, he said. I'd never felt more violated or ashamed in my life. It was around this time that I came across Edvard Munch's *Madonna* in an artbook, her bare breasts raised heavenward in hellish ecstasy. Emerging from the black background of Munch's canvas, the Holy Mother seemed to be saying that there was another, darker world than this one in which I lived, in which the ruthless aseptic light of purity ceaselessly shone, obliterating everything it touched. In this world—her world—an altogether different set of laws applied, the law of no law, where the very mother of God Himself could walk naked through the night and not be ashamed. Nothing resulted from the phone call.

Other than in art itself, I had no idea where that world might be. Nor did I know how to get there without being destroyed in the process. Guilt and shame, or so I then thought, must be the very preconditions for accommodating oneself to God, who so loves us that He demands our constant repentance for our sins, particularly those of a sexual nature. During certain periods of my grandfather's sickness, which is what we in my family called his combined violence and despair, I would walk up the hill to the house he lived in with my grandmother and spend the night there, partly in order to keep him from deploying the fruits of his so-called sickness against my grandmother and partly, if not more so, because their spare bedroom contained a television which I could use, long after they had gone unhappily to bed, to troll for any programming which might contain moving pictures of parts of the female body which were otherwise forbidden to my eyes. One night I hit the jackpot—the French film mentioned earlier, François Ozon's *Swimming Pool*—but I was so overwhelmed by the shot of Ludivine Sagnier naked in the bathtub that the moment I saw her bare breasts, I looked away out of fear of seeing her genitals. I hated myself for looking, hated myself for wanting to look, hated myself most of all for looking away—and for having done so at the precise moment when a great mystery would've been revealed, which might now be described as a glimpse at the unqualified universe. Years later I would learn that Sagnier's unqualified universe was obscured by soap bubbles, and I thought: too bad.

Why am I writing this? To what purpose and what end, or so I have had frequent occasion to ask myself over the course of drafting the initial versions of these pages, have I discussed at such length these details of both my past and current sexual being? While the former remains embarrassing—because so benign, naïve, cowardly—and frequently even humiliating to ponder, I am equally aware that the latter contains aspects which, though infinitely more tame than the perversions of a Sade or any number of twentieth or twenty-first century degenerates or even, perhaps, many so-called normal people who've grown up outside of a context of crushing religious fervor and fundamentalist law, nevertheless contains elements which many readers may find amoral at best and repulsive at worst, especially to those who have never considered paying a woman residing in a poverty-stricken Latin American country far south of the equator to bind herself with a ball gag or gag ball as she herself called it and touch herself while they watched. Even if these theoretical readers *had* actually made exactly this or similar requests of young women in distant countries, it seems unlikely to me that most if any of them would both openly admit to and then graphically describe doing so in a text meant for eventual public consumption, which would doubtless incur embarrassment and disgust on the part of certain members of their friends and family (the Biblical phrase is *to heap shame upon one's own house*) and perhaps even lead to their being fired from their position of employment. There is an element of risk in this. At the same time, in writing this I have had occasion to ask whether I would do such work myself as binding myself with a gag and exposing myself for the all-seeing camera, and the answer (so far) is no, because (or so I tell myself) I have already spent too much time under the gaze of the all-seeing eye which belongs, so I was told from earliest childhood, to that Being who, having set the earth spinning through the eternal darkness of space and even going so far as to place us there upon its rough-hewn and unforgiving surface, is both omniscient on the one hand and omnipresent on the other. It now seems to me no more inherently humiliating in order to make it possible to have food to eat and to keep the heat on to be paid to tie on a ball gag before a screen than it is to make sandwiches or be a fry cook or sell drinks at live sporting events or do data entry or deliver pizzas or be a concierge at a hotel or write descriptions of lawn ornaments and bedsheets for a tech startup's website, all of which I have done for the bare minimum wage and nearly all of which I found to be unpleasant, humiliating, and soul-sucking. There is no doubt in my mind that I would have discovered more about my own pleasure had I spent the same amount of time instead binding and gagging myself in front of a camera than in doing any of the abovementioned jobs. It's very likely that the same cowardice which caused me to look away from

Ludivine Sagnier's naked body is the one that makes me likelier to take up any of the above jobs again than to expose myself on camera. As is clear from these pages, I lack bravery and it is exactly bravery that I admire so much in sex workers. They expose themselves in order to make a life for themselves. In so doing they give pleasure to others. These pages such as they are are my exposure.

It is increasingly my suspicion that the urge to make art and the urge to expose oneself emanate from the same place: it's a wonder that more artists are not caught fucking in public parks, masturbating beneath overpasses, and generally fornicating on the canvases and even with the sculptures at gallery openings. Making art affords the artist a kind of lawful indecent exposure but this does not make the artist any less wretched even as it elevates the cultural reception of the result of the impulse to do so. Having for many years not believed in a savior, my belief in that great work of smut, Munch's *Madonna,* has only increased.

My heart is not pure. Nor is my conscience clear. After all, a clear conscience is nothing more than certainty masquerading as morality, and certainty is itself the single greatest enabler and promoter of violence in the entire human arsenal. I have no doubt of the integrity nor the purity of my grandfather's stated desire to go home, six months before his death, after he and my grandmother had just moved—or rather *been* moved—into an assisted living facility, him in such an advanced state of dementia that he could not carry on more than two or three sentences' worth of conversation, when he threw my grandmother to the floor of their room and repeatedly kicked her, demanding: *Take me home*. From where I now sit writing at the wrought-iron table I can see the Christ-trees standing black against a purple-black sky like an augury of the void pressed against the greater void to come. It has rained on and off all night. Everything dripping, everything damp. This paragraph is the first I have written in almost four days. Today was the fifteenth of October. It is now the sixteenth, half-past midnight. My earlier attempt to write, made this afternoon here at the wrought-iron table where I have written most of the words in this account, or whatever it is, was obliterated by the heaviest feeling of depression I can recall since moving to this city in the middle of the state where my wife and I moved when our lives in the state where I was born became unlivable. With the exception of the excellent Mexican food we ate for dinner, there has not been a single pleasurable moment in this entire day, which I have passed looking into various screens, my chest heavy, barely breathing. Earlier this week I was found out.

Whether I was snitched on or snooped on I cannot tell. I'm inclined to believe it was the latter. My boss, the chair of the department at the community college here in Nashville where I have been teaching since August, emailed me on Tuesday to say that another instructor at the college had forwarded him the prompts I gave my students as instructions for their first essay of the semester. I am concerned about how well they will work with our student population, he wrote, and would like to meet with you to discuss them. The final line of his email: I believe there is a mismatch between your materials and our students. This is how I knew I was in real trouble or something close to it. Not *your* students: *our* students. For the purposes of their first essay, I'd given them several options of emphasis: either to write about *The Seventh Seal*, which I had assigned them to watch, or to meditate on an aphorism or single section contained in various readings given to them from Pascal's *Pensées*, a short collection of aphorisms by Cioran, an excerpt from a strange work by an Italian writer named Guido Ceronetti, and the book of Ecclesiastes. Up to the past week, my class, a first-year writing course, had taken notions of health and unwellness as its theme, with the aim of considering through the practice of writing how such notions are constructed as regards not merely physical health but that of the psyche, spirit, soul, and society. We began with Ecclesiastes, our first reading of the semester, which provided us with the question I have been asking my students all term: how to deal with the idea that to gain knowledge is to gather up sorrow. In this country we are inundated with the flagrantly false cliché that knowledge is power, but the fact is, or so I have said to my students, knowledge forms nothing if not the very foundations of suffering, and my students, or at least most of those who have spoken up during class, and the vast majority of whom are black, seem to agree with me. As I have written the initial versions of last two or three sentences the rain has begun to fall again, passing through the pinkish light of the streetlight to the left of the Christ-trees, sounding snare-taps against the surface of my umbrella. After class on the morning I got the email I waited in my car for almost an hour, lighting one cigarette off the other in a supermarket parking lot near campus. (There are no parks nearby and nowhere good to sit. Smoking is not allowed on any part of the campus itself. If caught and warned three times, a fourth infraction, or so I have read in the frightful tract given me when I paid for my parking pass, may lead to termination of employment.) At noon I went to see the chair.

In the chair's office I learned about several other things besides smoking apparently not allowed on campus. The chief of these seemed to be the treatment of one's students—or rather, as he'd taken pains to point out in his email, the college's students—as intelligent human beings. That, or so I quickly learned, was out. Classics of world cinema, too, or so the chair inferred, were also out. I mean, he said, leaning back at his desk chair, touching his rigidly combed hair as if to make sure it was still there upon his head, looking directly at me over his desk: *The Seventh Seal*? And *Pascal*? I'm a scholar of seventeenth century French literature, he said, repeating the name of that famous worrier. First-year writing, he said. Pascal, he said. (Third time.) I'm a scholar, he said again, pausing more heavily before saying again of what a scholar he was (seventeenth century French literature), and I must ask you, he said: On what basis have you assigned such material? And to a first-year class? I attempted to explain on what basis I had assigned such material, in the main citing the fact that when I was a student I had always admired professors who aimed over my head because this meant they were taking me seriously. I was trying, I said, to take my students seriously, and I wanted them to know it. I didn't understand the material myself, I said. I didn't *understand* Pascal. I looked the chair in the eye: Do *you* understand Pascal? The chair seemed not to understand the question, and sat staring at me blankly for a moment through his red-framed glasses, until he crossed his long thin legs and said: I can understand you trying to *aim high*... pausing for a long moment before launching into a disquisition on why I, a lowly adjunct, must not do this, *with this population*, he said, pausing again before adding: *our* students. He did not say *underprivileged Black kids*, taking care to add a capital letter to the second word of the phrase, as I'm sure he would have had he said it, but he may as well have. Almost as if it were something of an afterthought, the chair went on to tell me that there would almost certainly not be a place for me in the spring. Enrollment, or so the chair claimed, was way down. After this casual termination of my employment the chair elected to inform me in detail why my prompts were far too difficult (and thus inappropriate) for *our students*. If I were asked to come back in the summer or the following fall, said the chair, I would be ordered to teach one of the generic courses pre-approved by the department. I asked the chair if the reason for our meeting—that so-called *mismatch* between my materials and the college's students—was in fact the real reason there would be no place for me in the spring and, if eventually invited back, the reason I would be forced to use a pre-approved course. The chair said, vigorously shaking his head, on which not a hair moved even slightly: No relation. All adjuncts are supposed to use one, he said. (At no point during my hiring, all of a week before the semester began, had this information been given to me—in the very conversation in which he'd hired me, the chair had in fact told me the opposite.) *This* will never happen again, he said, waving his hand in the air. Against my will I noticed the length and grace of the fingers of his hand, without blemish despite his age, as if they had no connection to him at all. He repeated again that enrollment was down, indeed so far down that even some of *his* full-time instructors did not have full loads for the spring... very far down, yes, the chair said, speaking more quickly now, I should not see *any* correlation between *this* and my lack of teaching next semester... I neglected to point out that only six weeks ago he'd told me quite definitively that I would have work in the spring and even in the summer. In any case, the chair said, we would have to make the best of it for the rest of the semester. To that end, he explained, I would be assigned a course leader, with whom I would have to meet. This so-called course leader, or so said the chair, would help me *adjust* my course to keep it more in line with the needs of my students.

This course leader was a poet, or so said the chair, but despite this had a very fine attention to detail. He laughed nervously after saying this and again touched the hair on top of his head. It's stupid of me, the chair said, to imply that a poet might not have a fine attention to detail. What I mean is that the course leader is *creative*. A creative person. The chair leaned back in his chair and re-crossed his legs—a move obviously calculated to provide him with a more authoritative posture—and said that he trusted *his* full-time professors. *He* trusted *them* very much. So much, he said, that he, the chair, even though he was the chair, and as such was in a position of authority over them, might even call some of them friends. (For fuck's sake, I thought: the man is so insecure he feels the need to make me cognizant of the very *idea* that he might in fact *have friends*—fair enough, or so I now think, writing this.) My prompts had been texted to the chair, or so the chair said, by one of *his* full-time teachers, without my name on them, but he'd figured out who they, the prompts, belonged to, quickly enough, he said, with a cold little smile that appeared in one corner of his mouth. His eyes behind his red-framed glasses gleamed. It was at this moment that I first suspected the chair had not been texted by anyone, but had simply been snooping on my online course, where the prompt was freely available, though intended only for my students. Or rather the students of the college. He seemed proud of himself, as if, after having shitted all over my good judgment and torn apart my prompts and terminated my employment, that after all this, he, the chair, expected my congratulations on his sleuthing. Instead, speaking slowly, I said: How—*exactly*—did you figure out the prompts were mine? The chair seemed taken aback by the question. His answer was a long moment in coming. (I have neglected to add that this entire time he had had the online version of my course open on his computer screen, to which the chair apparently had total access, and that he'd earlier told me he'd looked through my gradebook, and that when he informed me of having looked through my gradebook he said, with the same cold mouth-corner of a smile, that it was a great thing that he had such access to each instructor's courses. I was not invited to give my opinion on this and so kept it to myself.) Finally, the chair answered my question, the words tumbling forth as if they wanted out of his mouth as quickly as possible: There weren't many other options, the chair said. He just knew. After all, he said, I have a PhD in literature. The chair smiled now with both mouth-corners, as if again expecting to be congratulated. I did not congratulate him. A moment later I left his office. Since that moment, until tonight, three days later, a lingering sense of violation not having left my conscious brain for long, I have written nothing. It now occurs to me that this sense of violation is not much different from one I felt after the phone call mentioned earlier.

Yesterday, the day before I began writing the initial versions of this and the immediately preceding paragraph, I took my son to a battlefield where, just over one hundred and fifty-seven years ago, over a thousand men were killed in the space of an utterly senseless hour while attempting to assault a fort. They faced such heavy enfilade fire from above, or so I recently read, that I don't think any of them actually made it *to* the fort, much less were able to attempt to scale its walls. My son and I walked among headstones beneath which lay the remains of many Confederate soldiers who had died only a few hundred yards from the cemetery itself, and headed up to an old plantation house which had been used as a field hospital on the day of the battle. There was apparently so much blood, or so I'd read, that the floors of the house remained stained to this day, but this my son and I did not go inside to see, chiefly because a sign next to the gate before the house said tickets were required to enter this section of the property, and we had no tickets. Affixed to the gate itself was another sign on which were written the words PAUSE AND REFLECT, and explained that many people had been enslaved here on this spot, and then those same people had been forced to endure an incredible battle. My son asked me to read the sign to him and I did. Afterward we turned to walk back toward the cemetery, stopping beneath an overhang next to the so-called gift-shop to use the water fountain there. An old man sitting on a bench a few feet away asked me to bring my son over to him. Please, he said. I hesitated for a moment. The man wore a cap denoting him as a Navy veteran of the Second World War. A cane lay across his knees. His skin looked like used butcher's paper, and was covered with small sores that looked like pieces of earwax. I fought the urge to stare. You should tell him, he said, slowly, firmly: You should tell that boy he is looking at someone who, when he was his age, saw Civil War soldiers in a parade. You should tell him, he said, as my son looked blankly up at him, to remember that he saw a man who saw men who fought in places like this one. There are not many of us left, he said. I asked him where he served. He gave a wan smile: I was in all the right places, he said. Across three wars I never did hear a shot fired in anger. As I write these words it is now half-past one in the morning. The rain as it falls through the streetlight reminds me of the night I saw snow falling through the streetlight across the street from the house in the city where my wife and I lived with our son before our lives there became intolerable and the thought I then had of how hell must be like snow through blue light falling.

I am writing now on a clear fall day, the afternoon after I wrote the preceding two paragraphs late into the night. My depression over the encounter with the chair has abated somewhat: the weather is as perfect as one could ask for in early fall, breezy and in the low sixties, a western sun shining against the far side of the street at the café where I write these words, the exact kind of October day which might have caused the poet who later jumped from the bridge over the Mississippi to write: *Fall comes to us as a prize / to rouse us to our fate*. It is the kind of weather capable of transforming the terror-inducing image of non-existence into one of eternity, returning to death its former dignity and power, the kind of fall afternoon when it is possible to imagine one's ashes spread not merely on any barren hill on any barren day, but rather among the hush of the falling of the year's first snow.

Ever since I first began writing this account just over eleven months ago I have wondered what to call it. For many months I simply referred to it by the date on which I wrote its first words: 22 11 20. It is not a journal, nor a diary proper, though it has characteristics of both forms, being derived mainly from the raw material of my lived life and my thought-life, occasionally jerking forward in a more traditionally narrative fashion, though doing so without resolving the problems raised by the narrative movements themselves. In its early pages it was full of numbers. Two days ago, in the Confederate cemetery, my son put his foot against a small numbered stone. Look Dad, he said. I told him to take his foot off it. When he failed to immediately remove it, I growled at him: *Take it off*, I said. He removed his foot. I knelt next to him and said I was sorry for growling. You must never put your foot on a headstone, I said. Why, he said, looking up at me with all the seriousness he could muster with his five years. We have to be respectful of these graves, I said. There are people under here. He pointed at the ground: They're under here? Yes, I said. Later, after we left the old veteran on the bench, as we were passing back through the cemetery, my son ordered another kid not to put her feet on the headstones. At the same time as I hushed him I flushed with pride. When I was a boy, in the cemetery where the murdered man and later my grandfather and later still my grandmother were interred, I'd been given a similar order. Do not step on the graves. At the front of the cemetery, housed in a tiny shed not unlike those used in some neighborhoods to house so-called free libraries, was a binder filled with laminated pages, a ledger explaining who was buried where. I pored over the names and collections of initials of those soldiers who'd come to this place one day late in the fall of 1864, not long after the destruction of that city, Atlanta, which many of them had fought to hold and lost in the name of that cause which Ulysses S. Grant later described as the worst for which any nation ever fought a war, most of them shot dead in the hell between the fields of this former plantation and the hill just beyond, atop which still stood the fortifications from which the artillery of the Northern troops had rained down upon them, ultimately opening for them a place in this ground. My son asked if we could go. I said yes.

It is now the twenty-fifth of October, a Monday, the 107th birthday of the poet who leapt from the bridge. In the picture I love most of him, of him with his daughter, the two of them can be seen climbing over the gap of a fence somewhere in Ireland, where he went to his finish his long poem *The Dream Songs*. The picture was taken in the late sixties. Berryman's little girl is about the same age as my son. She wears a woolen sweater and her bearded father stands behind her, his hands on the fence posts, his gaze directed down at her. I am not a good man, or so he wrote in the last months of his life, and won't ever be, directing his words to the entity he had come again to refer to as the Lord: *You ask too much,* he wrote. I don't know whether he still believed on the morning when he leapt and struck the frozen riverbank, dead on impact. Last Friday, in the city where my father took his father to that asylum called Laureate, only a few miles from which my wife and son and I lived before our lives there became intolerable, to which we traveled at the end of last week, and from which we have now returned, I saw again my friend the poet mentioned earlier in these pages. His life he said had become a darkness and he no longer wanted to be in it. All avenues seemed closed to him. Eminently qualified to teach writing, he had been again denied a position by the self-important halfwits in charge of the English department at the local university (my words, not his). His isolation from the world—from having no place in this city which was the world he lived in—Tulsa: wretched world—far from his family, without friends, without position, and without escape route, had reached a point, he said, in which he had become so isolated from himself that he hardly felt he had a self at all. I told him of my conversation with the chair and of my dismissal. What are we supposed to do, he said. We are reasonably good at writing, you and I, he said, and talking about reading and writing, and we want to help others do the same, and have a space ourselves to read and write, and this is all we want to do. But there is no place in the world for it, he said. I said that I didn't know what to do. He said he didn't know either. Toward the end of our conversation I asked him if he was suicidal. No, he said, I'm not yet suicidal, though I have a lot of suicidal ideation. The presence of that *yet* alarmed me. It's better to be able to say I don't want to be in my life, he said, than not to say it. He was driving his black car and I was in the passenger seat. The car passed southward through the early afternoon sunlight. It's better to be able to say these things than not to say them, he said again, otherwise the pressure to hold them within would be too much, and might even create the possibility of the actuality of the event, he said. It's curious, I said, repeating something I'd recently said to Elle: since I quit believing in God—once the certainty of eternity vanished—suicide has been *out*. I said this hoping he would agree with me, but while he indicated that he understood my reasoning, he failed to say that the same was the case with him. I told him I hoped things would get better for him. We exchanged our goodbyes and I got out of the car. It was the same kind of day I referenced in the penultimate paragraph before this one. A light breeze chased a broken styrofoam cup across the street. I watched my friend in his car turn and go in the direction of the cup, and then pass it, and then the cup as it scudded along behind his car, which vanished from sight. I wished then, and still wish, writing this, that I could have brought myself to tell him that I loved him and would not under any circumstances want to have to do without him in the world. I suppose what I love about the photograph of the poet who later leapt from the bridge is his gaze, directed not at the camera but at his daughter. In that gaze I think is love.

This morning, the twenty-seventh of October, exactly two weeks to the day after the meeting, I told my students about the conversation I'd had with the chair, about how I'd been informed in no uncertain terms that the material I had assigned them was too difficult, and about the phrase *a student population like this one,* which, I said, glancing around the room filled almost entirely with black students, was code. A young woman sitting in the third row said: We know. The graves of the slave owners occupied the highest point of a gentle rise and were nearest the house. These white people's stones, unlike those of the soldiers who lay on the other side of the enslaved, were of the grandest make and fashion in the entire cemetery, though many of them by now lay in a state of advanced disrepair, especially one in particular, an aboveground grave or false sarcophagus whose lid had broken apart and into which it was possible to look inside. My son and I both looked. He asked me if anyone was in there. I said I didn't think so. I said to my students that I thought they deserved the best material I could bring them. They indicated that this is what they wanted. A large granite stone, obviously erected fairly recently, stood in the black portion of the cemetery with two words etched upon it in all-caps. My son asked me to read it to him. It is now 5:25pm as I write the initial version of these words. Beyond my wrought-iron table, reaching out against the pale darkening sky, are the two trees I once thought were three, and have previously referred to in this account as the Christ-trees. Their green has turned to black. Void on void. Those men and women and children who'd anguished and worked and loved and hoped and been tortured and died on that land in forced captivity lay directly between the soldiers who fought for the so-called right to keep them enslaved and the white family that actually exercised that right. The position of their eternal rest: buried in the stony ground between the oppressor and his army.

The granite marker read: FOREVER UNCHAINED. The soldiers who lay beyond were commemorated only by small rectangular markers bearing nothing more than initials and numbers. They were buried according to state of origin, with larger markers denoting the state sections. More than four hundred soldiers all lay buried in one mass grave marked UNKNOWN. The austere stone on which this word was etched stood taller than all the rest. It was after spending a moment looking at this largest stone that I opened the ledger containing the names of the dead, or some of them, since none of the graves of the formerly enslaved were marked at all, and likewise not written in the book. My son said: Can we go?

Yesterday I did not write. Instead, during part of the time in which I intended to write, I gazed at my computer screen as a totally naked and very pregnant woman sat upon a large ball, bouncing slightly. I had an erection, very stiff, and started to stroke it, thinking: What is going on here? Why, of all things, is *this* turning me on? I did not know. It is true that my wife and I have been talking lately, off and on, usually when I have had several or many things to drink, about having another baby—but surely this does not account for the erotic charge lit inside my head or at least my dick by a woman in her thirty-fourth week of pregnancy. Again, I did not know and still do not know and really, when it comes right down to it, do not want to know. I'm sure the reader is grateful for these details. Writing this today, I still wish that I had written yesterday instead of masturbating while watching the woman sitting upon her ball, and wished it even as I was touching myself while watching her bouncing on the ball to start with, but then again, I learned something, though of value which may at best be described as dubious. To my son I said, Yes, and we went. On the way home he fell asleep. Today at noon I spoke via computer screen with the woman the chair had assigned to help me *adjust* to the needs of *this student population*. This woman's face appeared on the same screen as the body of the naked pregnant lady. She seemed to wish to appear casual, and maintained a friendly demeanor, taking some time before actually getting to her speech about *this student population*. She made the linguistically politic step of criticizing the local public school system instead of the students themselves, an adroit conversational maneuver that seemed practiced. She said: How can I say this in a PC way. As I write these words, sitting at a café, three Christian college students are praying with a homeless person sitting at the other end of the café patio. This homeless person once asked me to enter the store next door to the café to buy cigarettes for him. He'd been banned from the store, he confessed, in a way with which he seemed to hope to indicate the injustice of said banning, because he had used, as he put it, a *word* about one of the black employees there. I said: A word, huh, and told him to ask someone else. She told me she would love to help me with anything she could, and that if I had any questions, or anything I wanted to run past her, I could definitely do that. I could tell she wanted me to ask her a question about something, to seek some kind of counsel, because this would have made her feel useful in some way that went beyond surveillance, which she clearly did not want to see as her role in talking to me, but I did not want to ask her a question about something, or anything, because it was a humiliation to be forced to have the conversation in the first place, and I did not feel like giving her the satisfaction of aiding her conscience, so all I said was that I would keep the offer in mind. As I write this the students are no longer praying with the homeless man and the homeless man is eating what looks like ice cream from a cup. Because I was fully clothed and did not wish to get cum on my shirt, I stopped stroking myself right before I came. I said to my students that I'd been informed I wouldn't be invited back next semester, and told them that my boss had informed me that this had nothing to do with the material I'd assigned. A student sitting to my right said: They lying. The so-called course leader said again that she'd love to help me with anything she could. Three weeks ago I asked an African American stripper if I could touch her while she danced on me. Baby, she said, you can do anything you want.

The dance cost thirty dollars and I tipped the stripper the rest of the contents of my pocket, eight or ten dollars in single bills. Though I felt I owed her, I did not tip the pregnant woman. A white man just walked past the patio where I am writing this wearing a golden blow-up crown and a purple robe. Behind him walked several children, also in costume. It is two days until that so-called holiday on which children and increasingly adults dress up in all manner of costumes and eat candy. The stripper wore a black onesie and had what may accurately be described as an exceptional ass, on which I with immense gratitude placed my hands. (Professional help is sometimes the best help.) I have decided to call this my daybook. For years when in attendance at parties commemorating this so-called holiday I refused to dress up and, when asked what my costume was, made the lame joke that I came as myself. It is perhaps not worth again remarking that part of what is interesting about coming is that doing so for a moment relieves me of being who I am. What's more is that I generally do not even have to dress up for these occasions, neither in purple robe nor blow-up crown. Last night I shot the load which was in a sense first chambered by the pregnant woman, and this projectile, separating in flight, landed in part on the underside of my chin. Elle, who was lying beside me when this happened, laughed. Usually you get me, she said. This time you got yourself.

Daybook: a ledger. At the time of this writing I am thirty-one years old and the husband of but one woman, and have, as reported above, been baptized, which means I am technically eligible to be an elder or trustee in most protestant churches, especially those that do not require a written confession of faith. Recently I realized if not how to end this book then at least where to end it. I began this writing eleven months and eight days ago, exactly 342 days ago including this one, during the eleventh month of the first year of a particular event which began during the final days of the life my wife and I were living in the state where I was born, an event which, particularly when it began, forced us to stay within the four walls of our house at a time when it would've been better for the two of us—as an *us*—to be almost anywhere else. Those glasses that I described much earlier in these pages as digging into the skin behind my ears now rest upon the bridge of my nose. Though the right-hand lens still occasionally pops out of its frame, the frames no longer dig into my head, and each time this has happened I have had the good fortune or luck to be able to screw the lens back into place with a very small screwdriver on permanent loan from my father. There are four crumpled cigarette ends on the table beside my keyboard. A fifth is burning between the index and middle fingers of my left hand as I type. It was about two months ago that I for the first time set foot in what the black woman mentioned in the above paragraph referred to as a booty emporium. I had a hundred-sixty dollars and a pint of whiskey in my pocket and the blessing of Elle tucked in the inner recesses of my impure heart.

After paying the entry fee I walked down a dark passageway and, just after entering a room with a stage at the front and a woman dancing on its pole, ducked quickly into the men's restroom in order, I suppose, both to get my breath and to steel myself against the feeling of iniquity crowding in hotly around my ears, and to remind myself that no one was looking at me nor did they know about the feeling of iniquity. I needed to fully insinuate myself into the place, or so I thought while pissing into the urinal in the surprisingly clean restroom, and so, in order to accomplish this, I ordered a bottle of orange juice at the bar, changed three of my twenties for ones, and asked for a cup of ice. Right after I sat down, in the furthest row and slightly to the left of the stage, I poured myself a drink from the whiskey and the orange juice and took a sip, and right after this the woman mentioned in the above paragraph knelt next to my chair, giving me an unobstructed (read: excellent) view of her cleavage. She asked if I'd like a dance. I said I'd just arrived and needed a moment, I wanted to orient myself. She gave an expression that seemed to say: Your loss, buddy. But I knew there would be others and did not take it to heart. At the same time, to my astonishment, even though it was precisely what I'd expected, another woman, on the stage, was in the process of removing what little clothing as she had on. A moment later she was completely naked, in response to which fact my brain produced this sentence: *What a place!*—the very same thought, or so I now think, writing this, that I had upon first walking into a Major League Baseball stadium at age eight with my father, and very nearly the same sense of wonder, a wonder at how incredible it was that there was a place devoted to such things as this, not the throwing and hitting of a small round leather ball but of the admiration of the female form and the enjoyment of her erotic hospitality. Indeed, the whole time I was there, on my first sojourn to the so-called booty emporium, I could scarcely scrape a dimwitted grin from my face, a grin that at several points threatened to split my face in two. I thought of my first day on the campus of the college in that northwestern city, the fact of *people* after all those years of isolation in that house in the woods where

I was raised, the difference being that, instead of the possibility of talk and of friendship, here was the possibility of lust and gratification—not the lust of eternal damnation I'd known for my entire childhood but rather the simple lust I felt every day. This place—up on the stage a dark-skinned woman in a glow-in-the-dark bikini was becoming a dark-skinned woman no-longer-in-a-glow-in-the-dark-bikini—this place, I thought, it's fantastic. Yesterday I did not write.

After a while I got up and purchased another bottle of orange juice and refreshed my ice cup. As I was waiting at the bar to make my order, a very tall pale woman with long braided pigtails brushed past me to get behind the bar, apologizing profusely. I hadn't noticed her before. In addition to apologizing profusely she was sweating with just as much abundance and removing what looked like kneepads such as one might wear while skateboarding. I'm sorry, she said, I don't mean to be sweating at you. She looked like she'd just rolled up. She apologized again. I'm so sweaty, she said. I laughed and said there was more than enough room for both of us. I'm actually a stripper and not a server, she said, removing a kneepad. In the process of doing so she nearly fell. I can give you a lap dance in a minute if you want, she said, righting herself, but you're trying to order and I'm here sweating at you and nearly falling down so I wouldn't expect you to. When I responded by saying: Why not, she seemed genuinely surprised and a little charmed. All right, she said, getting on her heels, but I'm totally still sweating. Most people don't like sweat, she said. I said I didn't mind. She led me out of the room with the stage and down another long hallway I hadn't noticed before, to a larger and darker room which had an even bigger stage, with booths along the lengths of the walls. Have a seat here, she said, and I sat down. She told me how much the dance was and I said all right. Did I pay before or after? After is fine, she said. It was incredibly loud in the room, which was full of men and a few women sitting in the audience area below the stage. She asked me to set my feet apart. Don't wanna step on them, she said, and I realized that wearing my Birkenstocks had not been the best of ideas. This was my first time getting an actual lap dance, I said. I didn't know what the rules were. Really, she said, your first? Aw hell! She asked me what my name was. I said: Henri. She said: Ain't that a French name? Believe me, I said, it's not. I did not say that this was, after a fashion, what my granny called me when I was a boy of around the same age as when I first saw my uncle her son pound nails into the hooves of a horse while a light mist fell beyond the door of a barn. The word she called me was *ornery*. She pronounced it like the French name and now I use it sometimes to refer to myself.

I asked her if it was okay if I touched her. She hopped up onto the seat, placing her stiletto heels on either side of my legs, and said: Knees down is fine with me, and then proceeded to press her ass into my face. I caught the unmistakable aroma of pussy, and it struck me that this was the first such aroma, other than Elle's, that I had smelled in more than a decade. When she let me come up for air I asked her what her name was. Karma, she said, but that's not my real name. I didn't figure it was, I said. Karma, she said again. Some people think I'm saying pharma! I said: Like Big Pharma? What, she said. I said: Maybe Little Pharma? Her legs, when I touched them, were far hairier than I'd expected a stripper's to be, and this detail, like all the others about this woman, amused me utterly. My first paid-for lap dance was over. The thing that impressed me most about the entire interaction was that it only differed from the kind of conversation I have for years been having with baristas and bartenders in that the person whose service I was paying for was intermittently rubbing her ass in my face while we talked. The interaction was of a sexual nature, yes, but that was the most superficial part of it, or rather it only served as the pretext for it: an excuse for two human beings to talk while in close proximity to one another. Though I had at no point during the dance felt aroused, I nonetheless stepped away from the booth feeling like I was walking inside a rapidly ascending elevator. Karma struck me as a silly person, the whole interaction was a silly interaction, and I wanted to do it again, though of course I also wanted to do it in a not-silly way, and toward the end of the night, the dark-skinned woman with the glow-in-the-dark bikini granted me that wish, in a way that was not so silly. I, a boy, was silly then: *Awn-ree*.

My friend the poet is the author of a book in which he repeats over and over the line *I want something other than time*. His demand, and it is a demand, goes beyond the possible, goes beyond the world, but this is what a writer wants and this is why a writer writes. It isn't good for the writer to want something other than time just as it isn't good for anyone to want something other than time but the writer my friend wants it and what's more, he says so. The obstinance of the writer is that he has the audacity to demand it, and so he does demand it, but there is nothing other than time in time, and no world *for* any of us: only this world. *Go over there my voice says,* he writes, but he can't go over there because he is a writer and a writer, even if he desires neither place, is always both here *and* there. The writer can't be anywhere else. This is the writer's failure and also why the writer writes. The inability to be either here or there but always in both places at once—this is both the writer's failure and may also play a major part in how one might become so isolated from oneself that one no longer desires to be oneself, or rather no longer possesses the desire to have the experience of being oneself, for part of the pain of the experience derives from the fact that one is always both oneself *then* in time and *now* in time, a variation on the problem of being both here *and* there. I wrote the initial version of the words of this paragraph on the third of November. Now it is the fourth. This morning I drove my son to school and since then I have been writing at the café where I recently saw the white man wearing the purple robe and blow-up crown. Such a man, I think, can be here or even there as he chooses. He can wear a robe or crown and no one will laugh at him for doing so. That is his privilege. I can and will imagine that his inner life is a blood-strewn abattoir and that is mine.

A teacher of history once asked me who were we to question God. I told him we were the only people for it. If we don't, I said, who will. My father and I carried all his parents' things from a trailer in the parking lot of the so-called assisted-living facility up and into a dark and forlorn room on the second floor. We sweated in the July sun and carried everything his parents had brought with them. My grandfather, who in his later years almost exclusively ever called me by the name of whatever town or city I was living in at the time, asked me what I was doing there. I asked him what he was doing here. He said he didn't know. When I saw the man with the blow-up crown, a line from a favorite hymn from my childhood popped into my head. There is a crown, the song says, and you can win it, if you go in Jesus' name. If ones gives up one's crown and robe and place in the mansion of eternity, for what does one trade these amaranthine things? Sin in life and nothingness at its end and, just before that nothingness, a dark room like the one into which my father and I carried his father and mother's possessions, the room poorly lit and full of stale air with windows that could not be opened. Where, I wonder now, at that moment in the parking lot, not even knowing where he was nor why he was there, was my grandfather's crown? Where was my grandmother's? Where was the crown of the boy whose head he found in the ditch? When you are gone your ashes will only be ashes no matter where or on what day they are scattered. Or, if you so choose instead to be lowered into the ground, you will become, eventually, no matter the quality of your casket or hand-built coffin, indistinguishable from the soil in which you are buried, and one day the marker which bears your name will not even bear that. *Sine nomine,* all your marker will bear witness to will be the indifference of time and the organic unconcern of decay. As I have written the initial versions of the above sentences of this paragraph all the light has gone out of the Christ-trees. My hands are cold. We moved in all their things—their last things—and drove away. We left them there alone. Two days later he threw her to the floor and kicked her there and demanded for her to take him home. Once found by the nursing staff, she was taken to the hospital and he was driven in a straitjacket to a different building in the same facility reserved for persons wreathed as a mark of honor. I don't know what color slippers they gave him this time. Six months later he lay in a hospital bed and his mouth hung open and could not be shut. She held his hand there and wept.

As the days grow shorter so does the number of pages remaining in this account. This day has contained a full hour's less light than the day before it. And so it will go for most of the duration of the year, the light of each passing day less and less until the solstice and the celebration of the birth of that boy who would one day be nailed to a rough piece of wood on a bald hill outside Jerusalem, a scene so awful not even his father could bear to look at it. I do not really blame the eternal father for this. In the same situation, that is to say on the hill outside the holy city, I too would have looked away; I, too, would have hidden my divine shame much as I have spent my life hiding away my particular human shame, or so I think now, writing this. I do not regard the impulse to hide as being to my credit, though I do think it's intimately related to the reason I began writing this account to begin with, to get my shame out into the open, fully knowing it might be seen as nothing more than that: shame. All I hope is that the illumination I have attempted to cast upon it has transformed it somehow, so that the light of my days may grow longer, my hands warmer, my body more my body, my mind more my mind, my relation to myself more an actual relation and not, as it has been for much of my life, an abnegation. I wrote the initial versions of the preceding sentences of this paragraph four days ago. Now it is the tenth of the month, the eleventh of the year. An iridescent sheen of clouds, high and thin, covers the sky to the west from my vantage point at the wrought-iron table. It is late afternoon. Last night I paid a naked woman who I could see only through my computer screen but who could not see me to wear a ball gag. It did nothing for me. What, if anything, have I learned here—or failed to learn? I want, I think, to speak and be spoken to. I want to reach through the screen and enter that room and touch the human being there and be touched by that human being.

All these past three days, because of the intensification of a long-term pain in my side—the right side of my abdomen, to be precise—and an irregularity in my bowels, I have thought, morbidly though without ever quite reaching a state of hysterics, almost without ceasing, that my death is coming soon. During these three days I have either not written at all or have written very little. Just now, while reading John Cheever's son's introduction to his father's diaries here beneath the porch light at the wrought-iron table, it struck me that I could only imagine most of the people I know reading the things I have written here *after* my own death; I have been writing exactly the kind of book which most people would not want published unless they were dead—this book—and then, just now, as I was reading the introduction to Cheever's diaries, in which Cheever's son recounts the conversation he had with his father, a conversation in which his father said that his diaries should not be published until after his death, it occurred to me that it would be very interesting, even if only to me, after having spent all this time—for most of the past eight years with varying degrees of intensity, and very intensely for most of the past seventy-two hours—thinking that my death might be imminent, to release into the world exactly such a book as this one, which I would only feel truly comfortable having read by others after my passing, and not only to release it, but to do so *in my own name* while I was still alive and *stay alive*. Today I realized that this past Monday, the eighth of November, the day I became convinced my death was imminent, was the seventeenth anniversary of the day a dear friend, with whom I was in love, in the very late afternoon sent me a message telling me she was going to kill herself that night, and I ran out into the backyard of the house in which I would much later begin writing this account and told my father I must call her, and he said no, because he disapproved of our relationship, and we were supposed to be having a family night, and I responded to this denial by saying I *had* to call her, and when I talked back to him, by the firepit in the backyard in front of my mother and two young sisters, as the day swiftly turned to dusk, he slapped me so hard with his open hand that it turned my head. This happened on 8 November 2004. Now it is 11 November 2021. In eleven days this earth will have gone all the way around the sun since I began writing these pages and my grandfather will have been dead almost four years. The person I badly wanted to call did not manage to die. She in later years transitioned into they and now is he. Now he calls himself by a new name, which most of his family outright refuses to use. To declare oneself one's own is to run the risk of being no one's—but not *no one*.

On the second day after he died, after my father and mother and I drove down to the little town where I was raised and where my grandfather and grandmother lived for the better part of more than three decades, my grandmother fell so deathly ill that she had to be taken to the hospital on the other side of the state line via ambulance. My father rode with her and spent the entire day there at her bedside. Her husband's funeral was to take place the next day. We all thought she was going to die. That night I drove through the dark across the state line with my mother to exchange her for my father. He and I drove back through heavy rain, and when we got home I argued with him that he should change his clothes, for there was a powerful flu virus that year, and we were all certain my grandmother had it, and my sense, then as now, was always that anything bad can get worse, and so I argued with him like an overbearing idiot, and finally he assented and discarded his clothes and showered, and when he had finished and dressed we stood on the front porch of the house where he had raised me, and he wept as the rain fell and I embraced him, and I held him there for a long time as he cried into my shoulder. His father was dead and his mother, we thought, would be soon. He'd sat with her all day, two days after his father's death, and she was unresponsive, saying nothing, unconscious. Inside the house we saw there were no sheets on the master bed. I helped him put them on, and as I helped him stretch the corners into their places, something I had never done with him before, it seemed to me that we had never done together anything more intimate, the son helping the father who was at that moment more son than father himself, because he was now without a father. I hate doing this, he said. I said that I hated doing it, too. You never get the corner where it goes the first time. You're right, he said. The next afternoon, standing just below the baptismal font where the pastor had years before submersed me in an attempt to accommodate me fully to the being both he and I had then believed to be the creator of the universe, I read my grandfather's eulogy. Two years later, almost to the very day, I would stand in the same spot and read the eulogy I'd written for my grandmother. After I read it my grandfather's son-in-law spoke, and then his son my father spoke, and the pastor spoke, and then we drove in a slow procession to the graveside and I helped carry his body in his casket to the hole in the ground before the gravestone that he and my grandmother had picked out and set there more than a decade earlier. The hard winter sun shone down on all of us except him who lay there in the four-sided box. As I've written the initial version of the words of this paragraph my hands have gotten cold and the day has become night. As if subsumed by the darkness itself, the Christ-trees are nowhere to be seen.

At the graveside the pastor gave the various members of the funeral party a chance to speak. Many did. They all said that he was a good man. A very good man. No one from his immediate family spoke—that is, until the dead man's younger brother, my great-uncle, told us all a story. One day, he said, when he and his brother were in college, his brother came into the room wearing a pair of six shooters. Well, he said his brother said, what should we do with these. They decided, he said, to go out into the dormitory parking lot, and my great-uncle told all of us there assembled that his older brother who now lay in the four-sided box had taken a coin out of his pocket and handed it to his brother and told him to toss it into the air above his head, and that when he did this, my great-uncle said his brother had said, he would shoot it. And so I threw the coin into the air above my head, said my grandfather's brother, and lo and behold, he shot a hole right through that coin. We all laughed. That's who he was, my great-uncle said. I was filled with admiration for my grandfather's brother for telling this story, as much for the fact that it could not possibly be true as for the fact that it painted the clearest picture he could've had of who his brother had been to him, his brother who'd once lain face-down on a waterbed with a pistol pressed to his head until my father came in the heavy gray dawn to take it from his hand and afterward drove him to the mental hospital in the city where I myself would later live with my wife until we could no longer bear to live there, his brother who in that same city would throw his wife of more than six decades to the floor of that darkened final room and kick her, screaming for her to take him home. The pastor said a few words before the service ended and the assembly broke apart. Two years later, after I read my grandmother's eulogy, that same pastor who had years before lowered me into the water of the baptistry to accommodate me fully to the God whom we then both recognized as God took the stage and informed the assembled mourners that when we closed a casket in this world a door opened into heaven. I fought the urge to cry out that there was no door no heaven nor did he have any right to spread falsehoods about the reality of our grief nor the nature of eternity itself. I did not cry out.

It struck me last night while I was talking to Elle that I have been writing this account, at least in part, in order to find out what being dead is like. I know it's a futile gesture. As the character of Death says in the film which my white boss, the chair, seemed to think too good for my black students: *I have no secrets. I have nothing to tell.* There is no place in the world for us, I think, and no world after this one, even if such a world may be suggested by the strange reality enacted in our dreams. A few weeks after the funeral I dreamed that I stood smoking a cigarette with my grandfather's brother. We stood in late afternoon light on the north side of a dream street in a small town on the plains in the north of the state where we both were born. My grandfather's brother said something and I laughed. He went through a door into the building behind us, and when he did I turned and saw, standing alone on the south side of the street, in deep shadow, alone, my grandfather. He did not seem pleased to see me. A few years later he would again visit me while I slept, twice, and both times he would swell and both times he swelled he would burst. I still do not know if, in the opinion of the pastor, my grandfather's act of throwing my grandmother to the floor and kicking her mercilessly, or any of his many other similarly violent actions committed over several decades, caused him my grandfather to forfeit his robe and crown, which he in any case did not have with him in that final forlorn room into which my father and I moved him. I think it is fair to infer—since he the pastor kept my grandfather the abuser on as a deacon at the church long after he knew the treatment to which he, a so-called pillar of the community, subjected his wife in the long darkness of those nights in his red house on the high bluff above the river—that ultimately it did not.

I'm writing now on Saturday morning, 13 November, at the wrought-iron table. The air is perfectly cool and crisp; a few scattered clouds whitened by sun are slowly ambulating across the blue sky. Elle has just taken the boy to the drug store to get a shot. Today we will watch football and I will make us biscuits and sausage gravy to eat. Once the sun has gone down I will watch football with my father at his house. Afterward, my plan is to go to the house of ill repute, as Elle earlier this week suggested I do, and pay for the hospitality of a woman who is not my wife. That is my plan, but as the Son of Man somewhere in the Gospels says, Say thou not that thou will do this or that on this day. In eight days I plan to drive west with Elle and the boy and stay for a few nights in the house where I was raised and where much later, almost exactly a year ago now, I began writing the initial versions of the opening pages of this account on the night after hunting with my papa in one of his several white pickups, my first time in close to fifteen years, the truck crawling from pasture to pasture, rising and falling through mauve mare's tails and reddish sage grass, from open hayfield to darkened thicket at the speed of three or four miles an hour, dark coming on, his green-stocked 6.5mm Creedmoor placed barrel-down against the floorboard between us. I hope to see him and my granny who called me ornery and walk in the cemetery again, and go down to the place beside the river where I once thought I would one day like to end my life. Everything seems possible to me now, here at 11:03am at my wrought-iron table, where I am currently facing not the Christ-trees but a large live oak, in which ten thousand or more droplets of sunlight are caught in the dark orange and yellow and yellow-green leaves that remain, all of which are likely to fall by the end of the month or perhaps even by the time of our return. To my right I can see the tops of the Christ-trees. The one to my left and in the center bear no pinecones, but the thief who denied his maker is laden with them. This, like a naked woman on a stage, or familiar mountains glimpsed from far off, or even the sight of the masterwork of a melancholy Norwegian painter, pleases the eye. That which pleases the eye in turn soothes the spirit and eases the heart. I have not felt this happy in weeks.

Clarity of vision produces definition and definition produces meaning. This, or so I wrote last fall, is not always desirable. I no longer know if the second half of the first part of this statement is true. Definition provides clarity, yes, but clarity produces the illusion of certainty, and certainty, even though it may have everything to do with one's attitude toward it, has little to do with meaning itself. Certainty is nothing more than *therefore*. My grandfather loved me. My grandmother loved my grandfather. And feared him. I love Elle, and on Saturday night I went again, as predicted, to the den of iniquity and ran my hands up and down a young black woman's thighs, and asked her what constituted a good night on the stage. She said: When I get a lot of tips. I fear being found out, but I am also writing these words with the aim of being found out, in part because of my experience of the doubled life in others and in myself, and my corresponding belief that this life, the life of running down the hill headlong, leads only to darkness, and I, for my part, have had enough of darkness. I want human touch and human thoughts and a human life, which is to say both this life and not this life. She loved him and he beat her. One day when I was twelve I did a poor job of raking leaves and my father, who was apparently suffering a great deal of tension in his spirit, likely because of the actions of his own father, was able to find relief from that tension only by taking a two-by-four from the woodpile and striking his only son with it. More than two decades later, when my boy throws a fit and screams at me and hits me in the face, there are times when I grab him far too hard by the arms or shoulders and I know this hurts him and that it is ridiculous for me, a thirty-one-year-old adult man, to take hold of a child in such a way, but my hands move quickly and forcefully, as if they are not my own, though of course I know they are. If Pascal were alive today, I believe he would make the reverse of his famous wager: we may as well act as if there is no God in heaven, for if there is a God worth going to after we die, He will not mind the fact that we did not believe in Him.

I do not expect my skin cells to thank me for their brief time alive on earth when I slough them off. I do not expect them to worship me or to sing for me or to fear me. It is *I* who fears *them*. (This remains the great loss of dignity contained within the loss of faith: once one feared God. Now: cells.) I fear their perversion, the onset of cancer of the bowels, rectum, lungs, and if I returned to the old way of being, the fear of the Lord, I believe I would not fear so for my bowels, rectum, lungs—instead of death it would be hell I saw leering at me from the periphery of my vision or manifesting itself as a cold feeling in the pit of my stomach when I'd stayed up far, far too late and stood in the bathroom before the mirror, not looking at the mirror but rather at the faucet running into the unclean sink, terrified by the only certainty the future holds for me: water down a pipe into the dark. Go over there my voice says, my friend writes, but he can't go over there. In his journals Cheever writes that the idea is to get away from one place, but I never get away, he writes, I never reach another place.

In the first month of last year I began writing a manuscript called *The Open Marriage*. I was so afraid of and for this manuscript that I set a password on the file, something I had not done since I set a lock on my diary when I was fourteen. Early that March I wrote my will. During the previous summer I'd begun talking with my wife about my desire and discussing some ways in which that desire might be fulfilled and though there were times when these conversations did not seem damaging to our relationship, there were other moments, increasing all throughout that fall, when it seemed like nothing else. By the time February rolled around—the February of the year in which I began writing this account, my daybook, and in which the world itself shut down—I was beginning to see the extent of the damage these conversations had wrought, were wreaking, on our life together. I continued to write *The Open Marriage* all throughout the days when it seemed like our marriage would not open but rather die. (Why this impulse to bear witness to my own destruction? If nothing else: the desire to remain alive implied by the indestructability of the impulse.) Indeed, I continued writing it up until the day when it seemed like the death of our marriage could come at any hour, writing even on the very day following the one on which my wife threatened to leave with our son and go spend an indefinite amount of time with my parents—she said a week but I knew in my heart that any separation would be permanent—and I told her that under no circumstances could she leave with our son to go stay with my parents. If anyone was going to take our son and go stay with my parents, or so I then said, it would be me. This day, to which I referred many pages earlier in this account, was the crucial one. Everything would be over by the next day. On a video call my mother said: both of you come. You two are going insane in that house. And I said: We can't. We can't come. And my father's face appeared on the screen and he said: Try it. And I asked my wife if she wanted to try it and she said yes, let's try it, and that was the first thing we had agreed on in many days together alone with our son in that house. The next evening, the third of April, after she finished work, we got in the car with little baggies of paper towels soaked in rubbing alcohol and left the gray house and drove all through the night until we came to this city in the state where I always swore I'd never live. There, everything changed.

To this day I have no explanation for this, except to say that when we changed our context, when we were around people who loved us regardless of our struggle with ourselves and with each other, we began to talk again. Now, for the first time in months, when she spoke I heard her speaking, and when I spoke she heard me speaking, and when she touched me it was her touching me, and when I touched her it was me touching her, and not some monster, and it seemed as if the touch was *our* touch and the words were actually *our* words, which had not been the case for so long that it was actually frightening, and remains so, to think how close we came to pulling completely apart the lives we'd begun together. She'd been afraid I was trying to replace her. I'd been afraid that I was becoming a living falsehood, and that this falsehood would eventually replace my selfhood, and that this, with regard to who we were to each other, would end by replacing both of us. I could no longer not allow myself to know that I knew what I knew about myself. Now she was no longer the woman often referred to in these pages merely as my wife. Now she was Elle: herself.

Two months later she and I pulled back into the driveway of that gray house to pack up the things we'd left behind. The moment we opened the door I saw we'd abandoned there more than I'd imagined. Stepping into that house again felt like entering a room where an excruciating and lonely death has occurred—which, in a sense, was what had happened there. The air was rancid with dust and decay. Everything lay exactly where we'd left it in April. The last cup I drank coffee from before we fled the house still sat out on the green table on the back porch, full of tepid rainwater. The brown husks of a dozen cigarette butts moldered in the blue glass ashtray. A sock lay on the dining room floor. Dirty laundry almost two months undone listed in the hamper—slack sheets on our bed twisted in the manner of a strangled corpse—the whole house had become an echoing, airless vacuum. The dead air: a living metaphor for the purgatorial existence we'd endured the last two months we'd lived there, where the hatred we felt for each other, once we left, *did* die. That carcass of our hatred, it now strikes me, was precisely what we could smell. It was as if, on the second of April, we'd actually decided to flee the death of our love and now, on the twenty-fourth of May, we'd come upon its cadaver. Only a few moments passed before we found ourselves standing in the corner of the backyard furthest from the house. Barely able to breathe, I lit a cigarette. So did Elle. We agreed we could not stay there. Half an hour later we checked ourselves into a hotel. Earlier in this account I posited that the characters in both fictions and dreams are in fact living ghosts. In that house we found a dead one. It was us.

It's three days now since I last wrote. I can hear the sounds of crows cawing, of dead leaves clattering, as I sit here at the picnic table at the pond where I wrote some of the earliest words of this account and where as I wrote those words I could hear my son playing in the backyard of the house where I grew up. Earlier this afternoon I drove to the Octavia Cemetery, referred to earlier in this account as the cemetery to the north where I've never wished to be buried. For the first time I saw my name on a headstone. It was etched on the one belonging to my grandfather and grandmother, beneath the names of my father and mother and above those of my two sisters. I traced the lines of its letters with my fingers—so strange to see it there, chiseled into the stone, those letters which, brought together, make up my so-called real name. Those letters will outlast me, I thought. They will outlast everyone I love. Beside the headstone of my grandfather and grandmother was a new grave—I was startled to see it—for one of my former classmates from my earliest grade school days. It belonged to the boy. The one we rolled down the hill when I was six and he was four. Now he lay beneath a bed of gravel: 16 June 2020. As I made my way through the headstones I came across the grave of another person I did not know had died, or had forgotten had died: an older woman I often saw mowing her lawn well after dark with a cigarette clutched between her teeth, a woman who, though she'd known me all my childhood, never failed to call me by the wrong name. There were more graves of people I did know or had forgotten were dead: an old woman of ninety who'd gently flirted with me at church; her husband; an old couple I'd never liked. Then I came to the grave of the murdered man who'd always liked me. His name was Floyd Davis. At the base of his headstone stood a mostly full bottle of Old Granddad whiskey, bottled-in-bond.

A few graves over I found, etched into my papa's parents' stone, the names of their children and their children's spouses, several of whom no longer were their spouses and had not been for years. Near their grave was that of a pair of elderly cousins of mine, dead on the same day—I recalled it, the afternoon my granny and I came upon their smashed car, crushed by a semi at a crossing. As I drove away from the cemetery I saw the face of my classmate as he was that day we rolled him down the hill. I recalled the gangly way he had of running on the playground after school. I heard the sound of his voice when he would say the two syllables of my name. FRIEND TO ALL. What happened to him? I understood, then, as I drove down the highway which descends the long sloping foothills of the mountains toward the house of my childhood, that the cemetery itself had become my primary means of receiving news about my home town, and that this meant that the facts came divorced from their stories, and it was strangely moving to me, to think now that this classmate I'd helped roll down the hill as he laughed and we laughed, and with whom I'd run and played at recess for all of my early school days, dead for more than a year, lay buried in the next grave over from that of my grandmother and grandfather. His remains would be there for as long as they held together beneath that stone, and for as long as the stone stood there above him. I drove home—or rather back down the highway to the place I still think of as home. I am writing this now on the twenty-second day of November.

On the way home from the cemetery, on the dirt road that leads to my granny's childhood home and my own, as I drove past the unmown fields of my recently deceased great uncle, her sister's husband, I turned on a hauntingly spare piano piece which I have for many years associated with that stretch of dirt road between the highway and the house of my childhood. While the piece began to play, even though very little wind was blowing, I saw as I drove a whirlwind begin to turn in the road, suddenly spinning so fast that my eyes could barely apprehend it, kicking up dust and leaves and throwing them twenty or thirty feet into the air. I brought the car to a stop and watched it spin and twirl: it lasted fifteen, maybe twenty seconds, then banked sharply toward the fence beside the road and was gone. Dumbfounded, I looked around. The remaining leaves on the trees that lined the road barely moved. My eyes, looking through those gold-framed lenses, did not deceive me: only a few leaves were fluttering on their branches. Nothing more. I recalled that God had led the Israelites as a pillar of smoke by day and a pillar of fire by night. What I'd just seen was a pillar of dust. Had I seen God, I wondered. Had I seen his ghost.

The boy's name was Brady Lumpkin. The names of the couple killed at the crossroads were Zama and Arthur Hobby. My dead adopted cousin's name was John Patrick Blake. The boy in the photograph who looked out from it with burning eyes, my father's father, now buried next to the boy: his wife of more than sixty years called him Jim. He called her Patsy Ruth. Last night, my son and Elle and I ate dinner with my granny and papa. My son played and laughed at my granny while she tickled him. She asked him, as she'd asked me many years before, Aren't you ornery, you're just ornery, and she pronounced this word just like the French version of a certain name. After dinner I stood on their front porch and looked out into the night. Their house sits high on a bald hill and faces the mountains to the north. A not-quite full moon had risen in the dark sky to the east, and a gentle breeze was ringing my granny's heavy black chimes. Their sound seemed to hold the moment within itself. I thought of how, exactly one year earlier, I went hunting with my papa, and he told me what his son said he wanted done with his ashes on the day of the first snow of the year after his death.

Even though the mountains were at least fifteen miles distant, from my papa's porch I could see no lights to the north, no lights in that empty stretch of land belonging to no region, with its high hills and low mountains and clear streams and rivers which I inhabited for the first eighteen years of my life: it felt good to breathe in its cold air, as if in doing so I was breathing who I was back into myself. When I saw the mountains in the darkness it was as if I could see both myself as I was now and myself as I had been at the same time. What, if nothing else, or so I now think, writing this, have I been trying to glimpse through all these pages, if not exactly both these parts of myself? Later, after we'd gone back to the house in which I was raised and much later began writing this account, I stood on the side porch of the house in the dark and smoked and as I peered down toward the woods and the river beyond them I saw that I had written the kind of book which would only be of interest to anyone if it were written by some famous or at least quietly acclaimed author. I could claim neither title. And yet there I was, and here, in these pages, is the book. Those were my mountains I'd seen earlier, and that was my river I now heard through the darkened woods. This was my house. Three hundred sixty-five days had passed since I began writing my account. I was almost finished. On a distant hillside on the other side of the river, a pack of coyotes began to address themselves to the not-quite full moon. I stood in the dark and smoked and listened to them and recalled my papa telling me about the coyote (*kai-yoat*) exactly one year ago. I punched *him,* he said.

The next morning, this morning, I walked out of the backyard down to the path that follows the river. More than six months had passed since I last walked it. As I drew close to the place where for many years I planned to end my life, I saw that the trail now diverts up and to the left through the thick brush, away from the water. The original path, or what's left of it, is now the very edge of the riverbank, in some areas only five or six inches wide. I followed what remains of this path to the place where I'd long intended to die, but found that the place itself is now gone. The river has washed it away, borne it off towards the sea. No cemetery for me, I thought. When my spirit enters eternity's dark and unknown room, it won't be a room at all. It will be water: *that* water. Make me into ashes. Scatter my body in the river. I'm already there.

*22 November 2020 – 22 November 2021*
*Watson, OK – Nashville, TN – Watson, OK*

*for Laura*
*you come too*

## About the Author

Nathan Knapp lives in Nashville, Tennessee. His essays have previously appeared in the *Times Literary Supplement, Review 31, Music & Literature,* and elsewhere. *Daybook* is his first novel.

Milton Keynes UK
Ingram Content Group UK Ltd.
UKHW012127110424
440929UK00004B/141